IT SOUNDS LIKE GHOSTS!

The group walked up the carpeted stairway. Suddenly eerie piano music, a bit off-key, was heard.

"What's that?" cried Jessica, almost losing her balance.

"Oh, nothing," said Ruth airily. "Probably the vibrations of our footsteps set off that old player piano."

"Are you sure there aren't any ghosts here?" asked Peter bluntly, looking over the banister at the piano below. Just as Ruth said, the keys were moving up and down by themselves as if being played by invisible hands.

Suddenly, the sound of a gong clanging through the quiet house startled them. An old grandfather clock stood on the second floor landing, its pendulum swinging slowly, tolling out the hour.

"I thought no one lived here," said Jessica.

"No one does," said Ruth.

"Then who wound the clock?" asked Peter.

The loud and unmistakable bang of a door slamming caused them all to go rigid. . . .

Bantam Skylark Books of related interest
Ask your bookseller for the books you have missed

THIRTEEN MEANS MAGIC (Abracadabra #1)
  by Eve Becker

ALICE WHIPPLE IN WONDERLAND
  by Laurie Adams & Allison Coudert

ANNIE AND THE ANIMALS
  by Barbara Beasley Murphy

THE CASTLE IN THE ATTIC
  by Elizabeth Winthrop

GHOST A LA MODE by Judi Miller

THE GHOST IN THE THIRD ROW by Bruce Coville

THE GHOST WORE GRAY by Bruce Coville

GOING HOME by Nicholasa Mohr

HEY, DIDI DARLING by S.A. Kennedy

MISS KNOW IT ALL AND THE GOOD DAY MICE
  by Carol Beach York

THE ORPHAN GAME by Barbara Cohen

THE PICOLINIS by Anne Graham Estern

TROUBLE AT THE MINES by Doreen Rappaport

THE PICOLINIS AND THE HAUNTED HOUSE

ANNE GRAHAM ESTERN

Illustrated by Hal Frenck

A BANTAM SKYLARK BOOK®
NEW YORK · TORONTO · LONDON · SYDNEY · AUCKLAND

RL 4, 007–011

THE PICOLINIS AND THE HAUNTED HOUSE
A Bantam Skylark Book / December 1989

Skylark Books is a registered trademark of Bantam Books, a division of Bantam Doubleday Dell Publishing Group, Inc. Registered in U.S. Patent and Trademark Office and elsewhere.

ISBN 0-553-15771-X

Published simultaneously in the United States and Canada

Bantam Books are published by Bantam Books, a division of Bantam Doubleday Dell Publishing Group, Inc. Its trademark, consisting of the words "Bantam Books" and the portrayal of a rooster, is Registered in U.S. Patent and Trademark Office and in other countries. Marca Registrada. Bantam Books, 666 Fifth Avenue, New York, New York 10103.

PRINTED IN THE UNITED STATES OF AMERICA

O   0 9 8 7 6 5 4 3 2 1

To Neil
*with love and appreciation for his patience
and encouragement.*

CONTENTS

1

CRAMPED QUARTERS

The tiny furnishings of a Victorian dollhouse were spread out on the floor of the Blake family's living room. The five Picolini dolls who lived in the little house lay nearby. Ten-year-old Jessica Blake was lovingly dusting each piece of furniture before carefully placing it back inside the dollhouse.

Peter, her twelve-year-old brother, was trying to concentrate on a homework project about the Civil War. He, too, loved the six-inch-high Picolini dolls and their unusual home. His thoughts wandered back to the day when his family had purchased the dollhouse at a country auction. Clara Clapshaw, who was the former owner of the Picolinis, told them the story of how the dolls had come to be created. It was a wonderful tale that began back in the 1880s with a very real and very famous Italian circus family known as the Magnificent Picos. Grandpapa Pico, the grand maestro of the circus, had wanted to give his family a home. Since they traveled, he couldn't give them a real home, so he built the family a very small one that could travel along with them.

The circus's magician created a family of dolls called the Picolinis to live in the little house. Each doll was made to resemble a member of the real Pico family. The name Picolini, Clara Clapshaw had explained, means "little Pico" in Italian.

Peter smiled as he remembered how Clara Clapshaw had whispered to them, "The darnedest things happen when I tell my troubles to the dolls!" She had truly believed that the Picolinis were magical. And after owning the dolls for some time, both he and Jessica suspected that Clara might have been right.

It was difficult for Peter to keep his attention focused on the Civil War. He watched as Jessica dusted the tiny juggling pins which lined the roof. Up above, bright circus pennants flew from striped poles, and down below, carved dancing bears supported columns on either side of the front door. A round stained-glass window showed a portrait of a beloved circus elephant.

Most unusual of all was the attic. The upper floor of the dollhouse looked like a circus tent. A web of trapezes and rope ladders stretched from one end to the other. There were wooden stilts, trunks crammed with circus costumes, and in one corner a silver unicycle. The walls were papered with faded circus posters advertising the *FAMOUS FLYING PICOLINIS*. High above, a sleeping loft held five small beds. Tiny musical instruments hung from hooks under the sleeping loft. The whole house looked as much like a gaily painted circus wagon as it did a home.

The Picolini dolls were dressed in elaborate circus costumes. Carved in wood with features painted on, each doll had its own personality. There was Mama, a glamorous red-haired beauty who could read a crystal ball. Papa was a sad-looking clown in a baggy, polka-dotted suit with pom-

poms. Stout Grandpapa sported a magnificent handlebar mustache. As the grand maestro of the circus, Grandpapa wore a top hat and shiny black boots. He held a red megaphone, always ready to make an important announcement.

Curly-haired Tonino was a young and muscular acrobat in striped tights and a tank top. His bold appearance gave the impression that at any moment he was going to perform a hair-raising stunt. His younger sister, the graceful and delicate Selina, was a ballerina and bareback rider. She wore a delicate skirt with tiny silk roses on it. Selina could stand on her toes with perfect balance. Her white horse, Nino, wore a red harness decorated with bells and ribbons. Nino was kept in a stable at the side of the dollhouse.

Wiping his glasses for a fresh look at his book, Peter dragged his thoughts back to the Civil War.

Jessica and Peter's mother was working in the living room too. An artist, she was painting on a large canvas at

her easel. Their father, an architect who was just now arriving home from his office, noted that his computer had been pushed far back into the corner to make room for all the activity.

"You'll all be happy to know," he said after greeting his family, "that we may not be living in such cramped quarters for much longer. You know we've been talking about moving to a larger space. Well, this past week I learned that the empty brownstone house across the street is finally for sale. I've had my eye on that one for a long time!"

"But that house is haunted!" exclaimed Jessica. "Everybody in the neighborhood knows that!"

"Come now, Jess," said Mr. Blake. "What makes you think that handsome house is haunted?"

Jessica didn't hesitate for a moment. "Strange noises come from it. It's dark and gloomy and sometimes lights go on and off, and . . ."

"There are supposed to be ghosts living there," finished Peter.

"Just because the shutters are drawn and the vines are overgrown doesn't mean it's haunted," said Mrs. Blake. "Remember that it has been empty for many years. A house needs constant care to keep it from appearing abandoned and, as you say, haunted. I was in that house once, many years ago, and I've never forgotten it. I would love to live there! I've walked by it a thousand times and thought how wonderful it would be to restore it to its former splendor. And I certainly have never seen signs of ghosts over there."

"If everybody thinks that the house is haunted," said Mr. Blake with a chuckle, "then we will get a good buy on it."

"You and Mom have been talking about our moving for a long time, but I didn't think it would be to a haunted house," complained Jessica.

"That house across the street is the perfect size for us," said Mr. Blake. "Surely you don't believe in haunted houses, and not here on Remsen Street in Brooklyn Heights, New York, in this day and age."

Jessica didn't want to answer her father. Instead she turned to her mother. "Why were you inside that house, Mom?" she asked.

"A letter was delivered to us by mistake and I brought it over there. The elderly woman who came to the door invited me in for a moment. I couldn't help admiring the fine architectural detail and the antique furniture in the house. The charm of the past still lingered there. When I told her how beautiful the house was, she showed me around the parlor floor. I fell in love with it right then and there. But at that time the house was not for sale."

"The relatives who inherited the house put it on the market just last week," said Mr. Blake.

"Probably because they heard it was haunted," muttered Peter.

"Enough," said Mrs. Blake, wiping her paintbrushes. "It's time to clean up. Mr. Winesack and Harvey are coming over for dinner. Peter, please set the table, and Jessica, after you've put the dollhouse back on the table, I'd like you to make one of your famous salads. I'll put the casserole into the oven."

"And I'll make the salad dressing," said Mr. Blake. "But first I intend to change into something more comfortable."

Jessica and Peter were delighted at the thought of seeing their old friend, Mr. Winesack, and his young assistant, Harvey. They often bicycled over to Mr. Winesack's antique shop just to chat.

Jessica lifted Mama Picolini carefully and smoothed out her blue satin gown. She draped an elegant silk shawl around the doll's shoulders and placed her in a comfortable-looking red velvet armchair. She polished Mama's crystal ball so that it sparkled, and she set it on the lace-covered dining table. Next, Tonino and Selina were placed against the mantelpiece. Grandpapa was seated next to Papa on the sofa.

"There now, Picolinis, your house is neat and clean again, all ready for our visitors," Jessica said, straightening the tiny painting of ocean and beach that hung over the mantelpiece.

"I would love to stay in our neighborhood, but not if it means moving to a house with ghosts!" said Peter, closing his book. "I wish there were a way to find out more about that house across the street."

"Why don't we ask Mr. Winesack to tell us something about it? He knows just about everything that ever happened around here," said Jessica, on her way to the kitchen to make the salad.

"Great idea," said Peter. He began to set out the forks and knives. "I know he won't think haunted houses are silly!"

2

MR. WINESACK'S STORY

"That was a most delicious meal, my dear Amelia, but I'm sure I couldn't eat another mouthful," said Mr. Winesack, refusing a fourth helping of Mrs. Blake's strawberry tart. It was difficult to believe that a man as thin and frail-looking as Mr. Winesack could manage to put away so much food.

"We were hoping you could tell us something about the empty house across the street," said Peter.

Pulling his napkin out of his collar, Mr. Winesack dabbed the corners of his mouth. Then he took an ivory toothpick from his vest pocket and began to poke at his teeth. His blue eyes looked thoughtful.

"The house across the street. Which house?"

"Oh, you know, the one that's all shuttered up and looks abandoned. Since you've lived and worked here all your life, we thought you might know its history. The kids in the neighborhood say it's haunted," said Jessica.

"You must mean the old Bartlett house," Mr. Winesack said with a smile. "I don't know anything about its being haunted, but it has always seemed to be a melancholy house. Wouldn't surprise me at all if it were haunted!"

Peter looked at his father triumphantly, as if to say, See, here's an adult who believes us!

"Mr. Winesack, please tell us about it!" begged Jessica. Pushing her bangs out of her eyes, she propped her elbows on the table and waited.

"Jessica my dear, I'll be happy to tell you all I know. But, mind you, I'm sure I don't have the complete story of that house. Just a few facts, which I shall try my best to dredge up from the past."

"That's more than we know about it," said Peter.

"Let's see now," began Mr. Winesack, staring off into the far corner of the living room. "The house was built in the 1850s by old General Bartlett who fought in the Civil War."

"I'm studying about the Civil War in school," said Peter eagerly.

"Well then, my boy, you can come over to the shop and see some fine Civil War swords I've been collecting. We have a . . ."

"They want to hear about the Bartlett house," interrupted Mr. Winesack's assistant, Harvey, as he patted the older man's arm gently.

"Ah yes, the Bartlett house," said Mr. Winesack. "Let's see now. The general was an important abolitionist."

"What's that?" asked Jessica.

"An abolitionist," explained Peter, "was a person who wanted to abolish slavery. Black men, women, and children were brought here, mostly from Africa, against their will. They were sold to families who made them pick cotton and be servants."

"You have learned your history well," said Mr. Winesack. "In fact, this whole area of Brooklyn Heights was very active in the anti-slavery movement. Now, where was I? Oh yes. General Bartlett had a son who became a famous judge. I remember Judge Bartlett well, although I was still a small boy when he died. An imposing figure he was!" Mr. Winesack stared intently at the ceiling, as if he could still see the old judge standing over him.

"And then . . ." prompted Jessica.

"Well, the judge had two daughters. I believe their names were . . ." Mr. Winesack paused, shaking his hand dramatically, as if trying to stir up his memory. "They were . . . let me see . . . the names are on the tip of my tongue. Give me a moment."

Jessica watched Mr. Winesack's face closely, hoping that the names wouldn't take too long to appear on the tip of his tongue, so that he could continue with the story.

"Ah, now I remember," he finally said with satisfaction. "Lavinia and Florence! That's right, Lavinia and Florence Bartlett! In fact you may even remember Florence, the younger daughter. She died only about six or seven years ago."

"That's the nice old woman I told you about who showed me around her house. She always wore elegant old-fashioned clothing. She was very polite, but she never became friendly with any of the neighbors," said Mrs. Blake.

"What happened over there to make the house haunted?" asked Peter.

"I didn't exactly say that it was haunted. I said it was melancholy. You see," Mr. Winesack continued, "the mother of the two girls died at a young age, leaving the judge brokenhearted. People say that it changed his personality completely. That must have been about 1900. The judge never remarried. He raised the two girls himself, very strictly I might add. It was as though he had sentenced himself and the girls to a life of sadness. I seem to recall that one of the daughters was involved in some sort of scandal that was quickly hushed up. It was around that time that things seemed to get even more unhappy over there. I never did know what happened, but whatever it was, it left Lavinia, the older daughter, very stern and humorless. The only word that comes to mind to describe Florence is *sad*. Very sad. I always figured that whatever the scandal was that changed everything over there, it involved Florence the most, because not only did she appear to be so unhappy, she seemed so . . . so . . ." Mr. Winesack paused, searching for the right word. Jessica and Peter waited expectantly. "So . . . broken," he finally said.

Jessica was quiet for a moment, full of sympathy for the unhappy Florence. "What finally happened to the sisters?" she asked softly.

"After the judge died, the two girls stayed on in the house. They never married. Florence was said to have been a great beauty in her youth. But she never encouraged any of the young men who tried to call on her. The sisters went everywhere together. It was as though Lavinia, the elder, couldn't or wouldn't let Florence out of her sight. Why, she even spoke for her. They came into my shop often. One time I asked Florence if she would like to see some new bronzes I had gotten. One in particular seemed to catch her fancy. I can still see her now, tenderly holding a little statue of a ballet dancer. Lavinia very sharply said, 'We're not interested!' She pulled the statue from Florence's hand and just about yanked her out of the shop. Very sad indeed."

"Did anyone ever find out what their secret was?" asked Jessica.

"No, not that I know of. They lived very quietly, mostly keeping to themselves. Lavinia died first, around 1976 I believe, when she was in her nineties. Florence lived on in the house by herself until she passed away about six years ago."

"Who owns the house now?" asked Mr. Blake.

"A distant cousin inherited it. He closed it up until very recently, when it was put up for sale, as is, with all the furnishings." Mr. Winesack rolled his eyes upward and smiled as he imagined the wonderful antiques that were stored in the house.

"Those two ladies," he continued, "lived entirely in the past. Never threw anything out. Never bought anything new unless they absolutely had to. They even made their clothes from old dresses belonging to their grandmother or their mother."

"Nothing wrong with that. They must have been wonderful old fabrics," said Mrs. Blake, who loved collecting

antique clothes. She glanced fondly into their living room. There in the corner stood a dressmaker's dummy with her latest purchase, a pearl-encrusted dress from the 1920s.

"Not that they needed money, mind you," added Mr. Winesack. "They were just peculiar. After Lavinia died, Florence did go out a little more often, still looking elegant, but remote, as though she had forgotten how to be with people. Now, Harvey here," said Mr. Winesack, turning to his assistant who had been quietly eating his third piece of strawberry pie, "can tell you more. He was inside that house often."

All the Blakes turned toward Harvey in surprise. "That's right," Harvey began, swallowing the last bit of pie. "I remember that house well. I was very young, but I remember the place as if it were yesterday."

"How come you got to know the house so well?" asked Jessica.

"My mother used to clean the place for the Bartlett sisters," said Harvey. "She took me with her when there was no school so she could keep an eye on me. I know every inch of that house. Except"—and here Harvey paused mysteriously—"except for one room."

"One room that you never saw? Why was that?" asked Peter.

"I never did find out. Miss Florence wouldn't let my mother or me have so much as a peek inside. It was the third floor front bedroom. She kept it locked when she wasn't in it. And she was in it a lot. Sometimes when she thought we were downstairs, I could hear music coming from that bedroom. It sounded to me like, of all things, circus music! I figured it had to be coming from a record on an old Victrola. What I couldn't figure out was why anyone would be playing circus music behind a locked door."

Jessica was about to ask Harvey another question when a loud crash was heard.

"That came from the dollhouse!" said Jessica, rushing over to see what had happened. "It's Mama Picolini." The doll had fallen off her chair and was lying on the floor beside it.

"Now, Jessica," Mr. Winesack said, "you must take better care of the Picolinis. They are not mere toys, they are valuable antiques. Put them away more carefully when you are through playing with them."

"I thought I had," said Jessica. Smoothing the doll's red hair, she crooned, "There now, Mama Picolini, you are just fine." Jessica held up the doll to show the others. "See? Nothing is broken."

"Mama Picolini looks almost as surprised as we were," said Peter, laughing.

"Oh, I nearly forgot," said Mr. Winesack, reaching into his pocket. "I brought your Picolinis a present." He handed Jessica a tiny tissue-wrapped package.

Jessica carefully put Mama Picolini back into the dollhouse. She unwrapped the tissue to reveal a small brass cylinder and some tiny brass tubes.

"It's a miniature telescope with its own tripod!" exclaimed Peter, taking the pieces and fitting them together.

"And it really works," said Harvey. "You can see quite a distance with it. That is, if you have a small enough eye to see through it!"

"Why, it's wonderful! Thank you," said Jessica, placing the telescope in the dollhouse beside one of the windows. Standing Tonino in front of it, she said, "Now, Tonino, you can watch the house across the street. Tell us if there are any strange goings-on."

"I'm glad you like it, my dear. I thought of the Picolinis the moment I saw it," said Mr. Winesack. "And now," he said as he stood up, "it's time for us to leave. It's almost past my bedtime!"

3

CAN IT BE?

Inside the dollhouse, the Picolinis sat frozen in silence as the Blake family cleared the table, washed the dishes, and finally went upstairs to bed. The minute the last sleepy goodnights were said, a faint glow appeared in the doll-house. The Picolinis began to move about excitedly. Every-one spoke at once. The usually calm dollhouse became a madhouse!

"Stop, everyone!" shouted Grandpapa through his megaphone. "Quiet down so I can think!"

"But can it be . . . ?"

"Is it possible . . . ?"

"Do we dare even think it . . . ?"

Grandpapa put down his megaphone and motioned for the dolls to take their seats. When they had all calmed down a bit, he began to speak.

"I realize that you are all excited. I, too, am excited. However, we must keep our wits about us so we can analyze the situation at hand. We must not ever get so out of control that we forget ourselves and do things like . . ." he glared at Mama Picolini, "like falling off chairs in front of the big folks!"

"But Grandpapa, do you realize that the sad Florence Bartlett may very well have been our own Flossie Barr!" said Mama. "I got so excited at the thought, I couldn't help myself. I felt lightheaded."

"Mama is right! As I listened to Mr. Winesack's story, I found myself thinking about our darling Flossie. She may actually have run away from that very house across the street when she was sixteen. That's how old she was when she joined our troupe, *the Magnificent Picos*!" said Papa.

"And that house may be the very one she was dragged back to so cruelly," said Selina.

"Harvey said he heard circus music coming from the room he never saw," said Papa.

"I wouldn't be surprised if Flossie continued to practice her routines in that room," added Selina. "That would be reason enough to need secrecy and circus music."

Mama nodded. "While it is hard to believe that such a coincidence could occur, it is within the realm of possibility. After all, stranger things have happened. Especially around us! I never thought I'd see or hear of Flossie again after that terrible night in Saratoga."

"Mama, what really did happen that night in Saratoga?" asked Tonino.

Mama dabbed at her eyes with her lace handkerchief. "It's not a story with a happy ending, *figlio mio*. It pains me to think about it. You tell it, Papa."

"I'll try to remember everything that happened," said Papa, adjusting the pom-poms on his clown suit so that he could sit more comfortably. "You see, the real Pico family became very attached to young Flossie Barr after she joined the circus. Mama and Papa Pico helped to train her. She was both beautiful and talented, and soon became the assistant to the strong man, Roberto Rossi."

Tonino picked Selina up and held her high over his head. "*Sì, sì,* I remember now. Roberto used to hoist Flossie up in the air like this!"

"Only Roberto could do it with just one hand," said Selina. Tonino stuck his tongue out at Selina as he put her down on the floor roughly. "Maybe he had a better partner!" he said sharply.

Ignoring Tonino, Selina gracefully pirouetted around the room. "I remember how Flossie stood in the palm of Roberto's hand and spun around like this." Selina ended in a deep bow in front of her family. Mama, Papa, and Grandpapa applauded, while Tonino continued to sulk.

"There was to be a wedding!" said Mama, putting her hand on Tonino's arm. "Flossie and Roberto fell in love. They were to be married after the last performance in Saratoga, New York," she sighed.

"What a busy time that was," added Grandpapa. "The whole circus troupe was involved in the wedding preparations. There were cakes with balloons flying from their centers. Miles and miles of pink ribbon were draped around the main tent. Even the horses had new satin rosettes under their ears!"

"The wedding cake was spectacular!" said Mama. "Three tiers of pink and white frosting with candy circus animals marching around each layer. At the very top, as a monument to everlasting love, stood the bride and groom, dolls just like us, made to resemble Roberto and Flossie. Grandpapa Pico had them created by the circus magician specially for the occasion."

"Did the Flossie and Roberto dolls have magic powers like us?" asked Selina.

"I don't know, *cara,*" said Mama. "You see, they were

whisked away after they were created. The paint on their faces was not even dry when they were set atop the cake!"

"And then," said Papa in a more somber tone, "just an hour before the wedding was to take place, Flossie's father and sister arrived uninvited! I do believe the sister's name was Lavinia. It had taken them two long years to locate Flossie. They dragged her away, giving her only a few minutes to pack up her things. Grandpapa Pico had just enough time to give Flossie the two dolls from the top of the cake. He wanted her to have a memento of her happy days with us."

"Roberto could do nothing to stop the family from taking her away because Flossie was not yet eighteen, legally underage," said Grandpapa. "And Grandpapa Pico couldn't stop them, either. After all, it was a father taking his daughter home. There was no way to keep her at the circus."

"Do you know," said Tonino, "those two dolls may be in the house across the street. That is, if Flossie Barr was Florence Bartlett. Didn't Mr. Winesack say that the two sisters never threw anything away?"

"Florence Bartlett would have cherished the Flossie and Roberto dolls," said Grandpapa.

"Florence's joining the circus must have been the scandal that was hushed up!" said Selina.

"And that's why Lavinia never let Florence out of her sight. She was afraid Florence would slip away again!" said Mama.

"It does all seem to fit together," said Papa, "but we have got to find out for sure. If it is true, then we have to get over there and search for those dolls. They belong with us, in our lovely home. The question is, how do we travel that distance?"

"We need a plan," said Tonino, doing cartwheels around the dining table. "What fun!"

"Yes," said Grandpapa. "We need a plan. But not now, because I believe I hear someone coming. We mustn't get so carried away by this turn of events that we run unnecessary risks. I would not want to lose our powers because we had been so careless that we let big people see us move. Back to your places!"

Grandpapa was right. Peter was sleepily walking down the stairs. Passing the dollhouse, he casually glanced down at it. Then he stopped and rubbed his eyes. Was he dreaming? Or did Papa really just slide into his chair? Were the dolls really magical? He and his sister once thought they heard circus music coming from the dollhouse. And they both thought they had felt real tears on Mama's face one day. But they had never seen the dolls actually move. Perhaps this was now his proof, Peter thought.

As he poured himself a glass of milk, he looked out the large windows of the living room. The maple tree in front of the brownstone was swaying gently in the night breeze. The leaves made playful shadows in the living room. It could have been the shadows of the leaves moving about the room that made him think he saw Papa move. He smiled at the possibility and, passing the dollhouse again on his way upstairs, patted the now still Papa doll on his head as he whispered, "Goodnight, Picolinis."

4

THE BARTLETT GENEALOGY

Jessica poured herself a generous helping of cereal at the breakfast table the next morning. "I wonder what the family scandal was," she mused, as she sliced a banana over her cereal.

"What scandal?" asked Peter, who was busy writing something down between mouthfuls of his cereal.

"The one Mr. Winesack mentioned last night at dinner. Don't you remember? He said there was a rumor that there was some sort of scandal involving the Bartlett sisters. Do you suppose it had to do with murder?" Jessica's brown eyes opened wide at the thought.

"More likely it was a disappointed love affair. Maybe one of the sisters was stood up at the altar! I wonder why neither one of them got married. In those days, girls were brought up to get married and have children," said Peter, without looking up from the paper he was working on.

"Isn't it great that you can do everything these days? Like Mom!" Jessica nodded appreciatively at her artist mother. Jessica finished her cereal and handed her hair-brush to Mrs. Blake, who began to braid Jessica's long brown hair.

Mrs. Blake smiled. "It just requires a bit of juggling and a lot of help from my family to keep it all going smoothly," she said. "I must admit that it would be a little easier for all of us if we had more space to live and work in."

"When do we get to see the haunted house, Dad?" asked Peter.

"Looks like we'll get to see the place sooner than I expected," said Mr. Blake, joining the others at the breakfast table. "I just called the real estate agent. She made an appointment with us for Saturday."

"That's three days away. I can hardly wait!" said Peter.

"I hope it's really not haunted and we buy it," said Jessica.

"We have to be prepared to make a quick decision, Amelia," Mr. Blake said to his wife. "The agent says that there are three men who want to use the house for their business headquarters. She would rather see a family get it so that the house can continue to be used as a home, but she will accept the first good offer she gets. So, my dear, if we really do like this house, we will have little time to linger over a decision."

"Oh, Christopher, I hate to be rushed into anything," said Mrs. Blake.

"Can we really live in the house if it's haunted?" asked Jessica, with a small shiver.

"Jess, when we go there on Saturday, you will see how normal a house it is. It will need a lot of work, but not the kind of work that involves getting rid of ghosts," said Mrs. Blake as she finished braiding Jessica's hair. Turning to Peter, she said, "You will have to get going if you want to get to school on time. Is that homework you are doing?"

Peter proudly held up the paper he had been writing. "It's the Bartlett family genealogy! At least, as much as I can determine from what Mr. Winesack told us last night. I thought it would be fun to figure out the dates of the family that once lived in the haunted house. It may not be entirely correct, but I'm sure it's pretty close."

"What's a genealogy?" asked Jessica.

"A genealogy," said Peter, "is a family history with the dates of birth, marriage, and death of all the members of the family."

Peter folded the paper carefully and slipped it between the salt and pepper shakers. "I'll show it to you after school. We have to hurry now," he said, putting on his jacket.

"I thought a genealogy had something to do with magic. Like, you know, a genie," said Jessica.

"Oh, Jess, don't you know anything at all? Come on, let's go." Peter grabbed his books and opened the front door. Jessica was close behind, grumbling about brothers who thought they knew everything.

Mr. Blake kissed his wife and followed the children out the door. In the sudden quiet of the apartment, Mrs. Blake lingered over her coffee. She glanced at the genealogy Peter had made. Smiling at how carefully he had figured out the probable ages of Lavinia and Florence Bartlett, she picked up a pencil and made a minor adjustment on it before re-folding it and setting it back between the salt and pepper shakers.

"How silly this is," she said to herself. "Here I am, a grown woman, becoming fascinated by the romance and history of a house we may or may not buy. I just wish the children would stop calling it 'the haunted house.'"

Mrs. Blake got up from the table and walked over to the front windows of the apartment to look across the street. In the morning sunlight, all looked serene behind the tangle of vines that had grown all around. Her eyes traveled slowly up the facade of the house. *The second floor would be for our bedrooms, and the third floor would be for my studio and Christopher's workroom,* she thought to herself. Her eyes lingered on the broken slats of the shuttered third floor windows. *We can repair those lovely old shutters so that they'll look as good as when they were installed.* Suddenly her expression changed. Something or someone was in the front room. Shadowy forms flitted about behind the shutters. "Good heavens," Mrs. Blake said aloud, "I am taking this haunted house idea too seriously. It's probably only the real estate agent showing the house to someone." With that, she went back to the table and wrote out her shopping list. Putting thoughts of haunted houses aside, she, too, left the apartment.

5

PROOF, BUT STILL NOT POSITIVE

The moment Mrs. Blake closed the door behind her, Mama raised her eyebrows. Like the starting gun at the races, it was the signal for the Picolinis to spring into action.

Selina rose from the sofa right onto the toes of her pink satin ballet shoes. Fluffing up her gauzy skirt, she raised her arms in a graceful arc above her head. Swaying from side to side, she danced on pointe around the doll-house.

Tonino clasped his hands behind his head, making the muscles in his arms pop up and down like Ping-Pong balls. Neatly flipping into a handstand, he followed Selina as she pirouetted between the tables and chairs.

"What's the matter? What is it, Mama?" said Papa, who awakened with a start. "It's broad daylight! We don't usually move about in the sunshine!"

"I have been struggling through the night to work my crystal ball. Ever since we learned that Flossie Barr may have been brought to that house across the street, I have tried and tried but I cannot bring Flossie Barr or Florence Bartlett into my crystal ball. Why has my crystal ball suddenly failed me? Do you think I am losing my touch?"

"Of course not, Mama," said Papa soothingly. "Sometimes in the past you have had problems. But you always managed to overcome them. You must just keep trying."

"I have never had such difficulty before," complained Mama. "It must be incorrect information that I am giving the crystal ball. There has got to be something wrong with my signals!"

"Maybe the fact that the house is haunted has something to do with it," suggested Selina.

"Nonsense," replied Mama. "Even if there were ghosts, I should be able to contact them. At least I could in the past. I must be losing my power!" With that, poor Mama burst into tears.

"There, there, *Mama bella*," said Papa, putting Mama's shawl around her shoulders and patting her back gently. "Don't cry! You make us sad too."

"Maybe," suggested Tonino, "the family genealogy Peter created would help you with some more specific details for your signals."

"I do not like to think that I need the help of a mere youth from the big world to help me do my work," sniffled Mama.

"Peter is not such a simple youth," said Selina. "He is very smart!"

"Hear that!" said Tonino. "My sweet little sister still admires Peter."

"Leave her alone," said Papa, noticing the rosy blush

that tinted Selina's face. "We have more important things to concern us now. We must help Mama!"

"Perhaps," admitted Mama, "it would be useful to study the genealogy at close range. Perhaps I am missing some crucial bit of information." Mama tapped her chin with her ivory fan. "Not that I couldn't eventually get my crystal ball to work without it, you understand."

"Of course, Mama. I, too, would like to see the genealogy. We could approximate from the dates Peter wrote down just how old Florence Bartlett was when she left home. We know for sure that Flossie was sixteen when she came to join the Magnificent Picos," said Grandpapa.

"And what year was that?" asked Tonino.

"1906," stated Papa emphatically.

"Wrong! It was 1903," said Grandpapa, patting his round belly. "I remember very clearly because that was when I began getting stouter."

"Grandpapa, you were always fat. You must have been born fat," said Tonino.

"Not true, insolent boy!" Grandpapa rapped Tonino on his bottom with the megaphone. Tonino dropped to the floor and pretended to be in pain.

"Stop arguing, you two," said Papa, pulling Tonino to his feet. "I know that it was 1902 when Flossie came to us, because that's when Roberto joined the circus."

"1902, 1903, 1906, you are all wrong. . . . It was 1900. The real Selina could only have been five years old at the time. She wanted to be just like Flossie when she grew up, and Selina Pico was born in 1895. I ought to know, don't you think!" said Selina Picolini.

"Let's get hold of that genealogy and find out for certain," said Mama. "You can see now why I was having so much trouble finding the right questions to ask my crystal ball!"

"*Sì, sì, Mama bella*. You are correct as usual," said Grandpapa, patting Mama's red hair. "We will get the genealogy and see what Peter has figured out."

"I'll go fetch it," said Tonino, jumping up and cart-wheeling right out of the dollhouse. He quickly spiraled down the twisted leg of the table on which the dollhouse sat, and dashed over to the Blakes' dining table. His shoulders slumped as he looked hopelessly up at the tabletop, which seemed to be such an enormous distance from the floor.

"The chair," shouted Grandpapa through his megaphone. "Move the chair over to the table!"

"*Sì, sì*, the chair," said Tonino, "just what I was about to do." Planting himself behind one of the cane-backed dining chairs, he began to push with all his might. Slowly the chair inched closer to the table. Tonino then pulled himself up the slippery chrome leg until he reached the chair seat. It was just a short hop onto the tabletop.

The Picolinis, watching from the dollhouse, cheered loudly as Tonino ran across the table and pulled the folded paper from between the salt and pepper shakers.

"It would make more sense to read it to you from here. That way I won't have to bring it back," called Tonino.

"Exactly what I was about to suggest. That boy can read my mind!" said Grandpapa.

Spreading out the paper, Tonino weighted it down with the sugar bowl, and the salt and pepper shakers. Then, bowing to his admiring family, he stepped onto the paper. Clearing his throat with great importance, he began to read.

"1850s—House built. 1860—Gen. Bartlett fights in

the Civil War. 1865—A son is born. 1885—The son, in his twenties, marries, and becomes a judge."

"Ah," interrupted Mama, "married in his twenties, a perfect time to marry."

"Hush, Mama darling," said Papa, gently putting his finger on her tiny mouth.

"1886—Lavinia born."

"That's right," said Mama. "She would be the older sister."

"1889—Florence born. 1900—The mother of Florence and Lavinia dies."

"Poor babies, no more mama . . ."

"Shhh, Mama!" begged Selina.

"1976—Lavinia dies, age 90. 1981—Florence dies, age 92."

"So that would make the year Florence arrived at the circus 1905. Could the real Selina have been ten years old when Flossie arrived?" asked Selina.

"Of course, *cara,* just the age for a young girl to worship a sixteen-year-old!"

"1905! That's right. Now I remember. The real Tonino was twelve then. He adored Flossie Barr and followed her everywhere. Not until Flossie announced her engagement to Roberto Rossi did he stop."

"Such a long time ago! How could we have remembered so far back in time? Now come back quickly, Tonino. Mrs. Blake may return at any time," said Papa.

As Tonino worked his way down from the dining table, Mama solemnly turned to Papa and Grandpapa. "You realize, *famiglia mia,* that while it may not be absolutely accurate, the Bartlett family genealogy is just another bit of proof that Florence Bartlett and Flossie Barr were one and the same person!"

"One and the same person!" echoed Grandpapa.

"One and the same person," repeated Selina and Papa together.

Tonino, meanwhile, was hoisting himself back into the dollhouse, and not a moment too soon. The sound of a key being inserted in the front door lock meant, of course, that someone was returning home. The dolls dashed back to their places just as Mrs. Blake stepped inside. They sat staring innocently into space as if nothing at all had just taken place.

Mrs. Blake hung up her coat and walked toward the kitchen with a bag of groceries. Passing the dining table, she noticed the paper with the genealogy on it.

"How odd," she said to herself. "I thought I left it between the salt and pepper shakers. After I wrote on it, I am almost certain I put it back exactly where Peter left it." She tucked it again between the salt and pepper shakers. Laughing to herself, she said aloud, "My memory is beginning to play tricks on me! Or perhaps there really is a genie in genealogy!"

6

A DISCOVERY

"Raining!" exclaimed Jessica, as she looked out the front window on Saturday morning. "It was sunny all week when we had school. Not fair!"

"Can we keep our appointment to see the haunted house, Mom?" asked Peter.

"Why not? A little rain won't stop us. And how many times have I asked you please to stop calling it a haunted house. Since you can't go outside to bike or skate this morning, I suggest you begin a thorough cleanup of your rooms. A rainy day is perfect for getting rid of all the old toys and books you no longer want. You can pack everything up for giveaway and bring it down to the cellar. I put aside some cartons for you to use."

"Ugh, talk about boring!" complained Jessica.

"Mom, do we have to? I can think of lots of other things I'd rather do on a rainy day," said Peter.

"Your bedrooms, which are tiny to begin with, are so packed that I can hardly walk in them. Since we may be moving very soon, it would be a good idea to get a head start on packing," answered Mrs. Blake. "I'm going to start weeding out my things too."

Groaning loudly, the children reluctantly dragged the empty cartons upstairs and spent the next two hours sorting through all of the books and toys they'd accumulated. After deciding what she could part with, Jessica lugged a heavy carton into the hall and asked Peter to help her carry it down to the cellar. Peter had one of his own to bring down.

"The landlord gave us permission to put things in the front of the cellar, near the wall," called Mrs. Blake as the children pushed the boxes into the hallway. "He cleared space for us. I've unlocked the cellar door and turned the lights on for you," she added.

The two children hauled their cartons over to the front wall of the cellar. Wearily sitting down on her neatly packed box, Jessica pushed her bangs off her forehead and leaned back to rest against the wall. She looked at Peter's carton, too full to be closed properly. Reaching over, she pulled out a small book from the top of the box. "I remember this one, Peter. It's your old journal. You never would let me read it!"

"Give that to me, Jessica. I didn't mean to put that in. It's my private property!"

Jessica laughed as she opened the book and pretended to read.

Furious, Peter lunged for the book. Jessica clutched it tightly as he tried to pull it away. One good tug and the book flew from Jessica's hands. She lost her balance, toppled off the carton, and fell against the wall. Sensing that the wall seemed to move from the force of her body, she quickly turned to examine it more closely.

"Peter, there's a door! A small door! I thought I felt the wall move! And see, here's a handle!" she said, pointing to a wooden lever quite low on the wall. Tracing her finger along the peeling paint on the brick wall, she outlined a small wooden door painted to match the brick of the cellar wall.

"I've never noticed it before. But it's clearly a door!" agreed Peter.

"We never noticed it because there was always a lot of junk stored here. Now that it's been cleared out, you can see it! What I don't understand is why anyone would want a door here," Jessica said.

"Maybe it's only a closet. Or maybe . . . maybe it's a very important and historical door leading to something outside. I have an idea what it might be, but I'm afraid to get too excited about it until we open it and look inside," said Peter.

They pulled the small handle as hard as they could. The door groaned and creaked loudly, and then it swung open.

Cobwebs and dirt obscured an earthen cave. Wooden steps led down into darkness below. Old canning jars sat on sagging shelves on either side of the steps. As their eyes became accustomed to the darkness, the children could see that the steps led to a tunnel! It seemed to lead from their cellar and out underneath the street.

Very cautiously the children stepped down, testing each step as they went. The light from the cellar cast eerie shadows into the tunnel. The steps, like the door, creaked as if objecting to the children's presence.

The tunnel was about five feet high and seemed to be carved out of the earth below the street outside. Jessica edged into the darkness. Suddenly she stumbled and nearly fell. Glancing down, her heart froze when she saw in the dim light the pale skeleton of a four-legged creature the size of a large dog!

Shrieking hysterically, she turned and ran back into the cellar. Peter waited just long enough to find out what it was that had so frightened his sister before he, too, dashed back into the house.

"It was only a pile of old bones," he said. "Somebody must have buried a dog down here long ago. You don't have to be afraid of bones. They're harmless. What's more important, Jessica, is that I think we may have stumbled on a very exciting discovery!"

"A very exciting discovery. Old bones," said Jessica, feeling safer now that she was on familiar ground.

"Forget about the bones. We may have discovered a part of the Underground Railroad that was used to help slaves run to freedom during the Civil War. In school we learned that a network of tunnels runs under many of the

streets in Brooklyn Heights. We may have an entrance to a tunnel right here in our own cellar! Wouldn't it be great to explore it and find out where it leads?"

"Whatever you want to do," said Jessica, "do it without me. I'm not going down there. I'm getting out of here. I'm going upstairs!"

Mrs. Blake had lunch ready when the children came up from the cellar. Peter, thrilled with the prospect of having a bit of history right in their own cellar, was eager to tell his mother what they had just seen. Mrs. Blake, however, interrupted him and said, "Wash up first, and we'll hear about it at the table."

"This may be the most important discovery made in Brooklyn in years, and Mom says 'Wash up!'" complained Peter.

"Moms!" added Jessica.

7

THE VIEW THROUGH THE TELESCOPE

Inside the dollhouse, Mama Picolini sat stiffly in her chair at the lace-covered dining table. Cautiously she lifted her long-lashed violet eyes to get a better view of Jessica and Peter as they ate their sandwiches. Ever so slowly, she stretched out one of her legs. The pointed tip of her high-button shoe poked Papa, who was dozing comfortably. Startled, Papa arched his painted eyebrows into two black question marks. Noticing Mama's intense stare, Papa slowly and silently changed his position on the sofa the tiniest bit so that he could follow her gaze. He sensed the excitement in the air as the children's story tumbled out.

Papa elbowed Grandpapa who slid soundlessly to the end of the sofa so that he could nudge Selina. Poised gracefully on one toe, Selina silently pivoted just enough so that she, too, could peer at the children. Tonino, propped in front of the new telescope, remained motionless, concentrating on the house across the street.

Suddenly Tonino's mouth fell open. His painted lips

formed a perfect oval of surprise. His eyes blinked and his wooden nose twitched. He could hardly believe what he was seeing. Bursting to tell the others what was happening, his expression changed to one of pain as he realized that he couldn't make a sound. The Picolinis watched him nervously, fearful that he might, in his enthusiasm, give away their secret powers.

"What is it?" Mama's eyes questioned silently.

"Shadows," Tonino mouthed back.

Mama responded with another questioning look that meant, "So, what's so unusual about shadows?"

"Shadows," Tonino mouthed again. "Shadows that look like . . . that look like . . ." With his finger he gently tapped his own chest. "Like us!"

Mama couldn't figure out what Tonino was trying to say.

Frustrated, Tonino continued to stare, fascinated, into the telescope.

Meanwhile, Jessica and Peter were halfway through their sandwiches.

"Tell me more about the Underground Railroad," said Jessica.

"We learned in school that the Underground Railroad wasn't a real railroad at all. It was a network of people who helped slaves escape from slavery in the South. This was even before the Civil War started. Sometimes the runaway slaves were hidden in houses, sometimes in barns, or even in wagons, under supplies. They moved secretly from place to place, usually at night. It was rumored that tunnels were built under the streets here in Brooklyn. The tunnels led from some of the houses to a main tunnel, which then went down to the river where a boat would be waiting to take them to the river. From there it was only a short distance to Canada and freedom."

"You may be right, Peter. The tunnel you found in our cellar could have been constructed as a part of the Underground Railroad," said Mrs. Blake. "Brooklyn Heights, as Mr. Winesack told you the other night, was an area where there were very strong feelings against slavery."

"I know," said Peter. "We learned about Henry Ward Beecher, who was a famous preacher here in Brooklyn Heights at the time of the Civil War. We even went to see a statue of him in Cadman Park. Anyway, Henry Ward Beecher urged his congregation to do all they could to help the slaves get their freedom. Lots of famous politicians visited his church, Plymouth Church—even Abraham Lincoln. Our class went there too. It's on Hicks Street."

"I have heard that quite a few houses here in the Heights have tunnels in their basements. I wonder if a map of them exists somewhere," said Mrs. Blake.

"I doubt it," said Peter. "People kept the Underground Railroad very secret. There were laws against helping the slaves, even though the North was sympathetic to them. It was illegal to help a slave go from one state to another. So there are no written records of the Underground Railroad. Only rumor and the discovery of another tunnel under the streets every now and then."

"That's true," said Mrs. Blake. "While I have heard people in the neighborhood talk about the Underground Railroad, I've never actually seen anything written about the tunnels."

"The historian who showed us around the church said that the name Underground Railroad seems to have come from a Southern sheriff chasing a group of slaves trying to escape. The sheriff said that suddenly the slaves disappeared into the earth as though swallowed up by an underground railroad."

"So then, if you guessed right, we may have a part of that Underground Railroad right here under our house! What's it good for now?" asked Jessica.

"Nothing. Absolutely nothing," said Mrs. Blake. "Those tunnels were built before the 1860s. That's over a hundred and thirty years ago! They are probably filled in or caved in by now. They certainly wouldn't be safe to enter. If we really do have a tunnel leading from this house, I wouldn't want you two exploring it."

Jessica, having finished her sandwich, walked over to the dollhouse. "How about that, Picolinis? A piece of history right here in our own cellar." Jessica was about to reach inside and move one of the dolls, when she suddenly stopped. She looked from one member of the Picolini family to another. Something was very wrong. "Funny," she whispered, "I left Grandpapa and Papa resting peacefully on their sofa, and I placed Mama so that she could look into her crystal ball." Jessica turned to Peter. "Have you been playing with the dolls?"

Peter laughed. "Between cleaning out my room, putting the cartons down in the cellar, and making what may be a most important discovery, I didn't have time to play with the dollhouse. Why?"

"Well," Jessica began. She was interrupted by the doorbell. She ran to answer it and let in the real estate agent.

"Hello, hello! Is everybody ready to see one of the best-preserved houses in Brooklyn Heights?" the agent asked cheerfully.

"We certainly are," said Mr. Blake, coming downstairs and putting on his raincoat.

All other thoughts faded as the Blakes got ready to leave. In just a few minutes they were going to see the inside of the haunted house!

8

THE HOUSE ACROSS THE STREET

"You're all going to love this place," the real estate agent said as they crossed the rain-spattered street. "It's like stepping back one century. By the way," she added as she fumbled with the front door keys. "Let's not be formal. Call me Ruth." She held the elaborately carved wooden door open as the Blakes stepped inside.

They stood in the hallway until their eyes adjusted to the darkness. Even the daylight straying in from the windows seemed to be an intrusion. Jessica, usually the first to run ahead and explore, remained close to Peter and her parents.

Ruth felt her way until she found a lamp that worked. "Most of the lights here still operate on gas or kerosene. There were only a few electric lights ever installed in the house. You don't get to see gaslights very often in this day and age."

"Amazing!" said Mr. Blake as he stared at the fine old

moldings on the walls and the elegant plasterwork that decorated the ceilings.

An iron hat rack stood near the front door, with two old-fashioned straw bonnets and a ruffled silk parasol hanging on it as if they were on display in an antique store.

"I feel as though the Bartletts are still here, about to put on their hats and go out," said Jessica with a little shiver.

Mrs. Blake put her arm around her daughter and pointed to the Victorian furniture in the front parlor. "Look. They're the same as the velvet sofa and chairs in the Picolini house!"

"Not very inviting," said Peter as he poked the heavy layer of dust that covered the purple velvet upholstery. A few worn leatherbound books sat on a marble-topped table next to a box that had been painstakingly covered with tiny seashells. It was almost impossible to see the design of faded roses and vines in the worn carpet. A peeling but intricately carved gilt-framed mirror hung over the marble fireplace. On the mantelpiece stood a sculpted clock held up by golden angels.

"Ten to five," said Jessica, wondering what year the clock had finally given up ticking.

"It's always ten to five here," Ruth said with a laugh.

Mrs. Blake picked up one of the books and blew a puff of dust off before opening it. "Lavinia Bartlett, 1922," she read from the inside cover.

"Everything is exactly as they left it," said Ruth, patting the upright player piano that stood in the corner. "When the younger Miss Bartlett died, there was no one around to straighten out or to pack up. The cousin who inherited the house said 'Sell it—lock, stock, and barrel.' The estate was tied up in the courts until very recently. We could only start showing it a few days ago. What a find for the people who buy this place! Everything here is original, with no distressing renovations to mar the beauty. I really don't want to seem pushy, but if you like old houses, I think this place is a steal."

Mr. Blake nodded. He seemed to be in complete agreement with the agent.

The group walked up the carpeted stairway, stopping at a niche in the wall to admire a bronze statue of a goddess holding a bow and arrow. Suddenly eerie piano music, a bit off-key, was heard.

"What's that?" cried Jessica, almost losing her balance.

"Oh, nothing," said Ruth airily. She readjusted her scarf slowly, as if considering what to say. "Probably the vibrations of our footsteps set that old player piano off."

"Are you sure there aren't any ghosts here?" asked Peter bluntly, looking over the banister at the piano below. Just as Ruth said, the keys were moving up and down by themselves as if being played by invisible hands.

"There are no ghosts here," said Mr. Blake firmly, as the music faded and the keys finally settled down.

"I wish I had your courage," whispered Mrs. Blake to her husband. Timidly she opened a closet door at the landing. Inside was a row of old-fashioned silk dresses with lace collars and tiny black buttons. "Why, these are wonderful," she exclaimed. "An entire wardrobe from the 1890s! What a treasure."

Suddenly, the sound of a gong clanging through the quiet house startled them. Looking around, Peter found the source. An old grandfather clock stood on the second floor landing, its pendulum swinging slowly, tolling out the hour.

"I thought no one lived here," said Jessica.

"No one does," said the agent.

"Then who wound the clock?" asked Peter.

"Old mechanisms, you know, respond to every little

vibration. Five of us walking up this creaky stairway could do it. Nothing to be frightened of," said Ruth, who was beginning to sound just a bit skeptical herself.

The loud and unmistakable bang of a door slamming caused them all to go rigid. "What was that!" cried Jessica, grabbing her father's hand.

"I thought we were the only ones in the house," said Peter.

Ruth nervously adjusted her hair as she tried to compose herself. "You're all so jumpy. You're forgetting that this is an old and drafty house. We left some doors open when we were downstairs. Probably the wind caused one of them to slam shut. There is nothing to worry about."

"She could be right. Vibrations and drafts can cause odd things to happen," said Mr. Blake to his wife. "After all, noises can't hurt us!"

It was obvious that Mr. Blake was so thoroughly charmed with what he had seen so far that he wasn't going to be put off by these unusual sounds. To the great relief of the real estate agent, Mr. Blake suggested that they continue.

9

WHAT THE CRYSTAL BALL REVEALED

The moment the Blakes left their apartment with the real estate agent, the Picolinis crowded around Tonino. He smiled shyly as he realized that he had become the center of attention.

"What have you seen over there!"

"Hurry, tell us!"

Tonino stepped away from the telescope and, with a grand flourish, said, "See for yourself."

One by one, the Picolinis came up and peered through the eyepiece. The wooden shutters in the house across the street were brought into close focus by the little telescope, but no one could see anything unusual.

"Tonino, how could you do this to me! I got so excited, but I see nothing, absolutely nothing in this useless telescope," said Mama in a very disappointed voice. "And to tease us at a time like this, when my crystal ball doesn't seem to be working. How could you!"

"You have been fooling around with us, my boy!" shouted Papa. "I see nothing remarkable over there!"

"We'll never believe anything you say again," said Selina, annoyed with her brother for getting their hopes up.

"But I saw something. I most certainly did. I saw shadows moving back and forth," wailed Tonino. "Shadows of little people just like us! I thought I'd found . . . Flossie and Roberto!"

"So where are they now?" asked Grandpapa in a stern voice.

Mama, meanwhile, reached for her crystal ball. "I know that I have been having difficulty lately conjuring up Flossie Barr. But perhaps there is no Flossie Barr over there. I shall try again, only this time I shall concentrate on the Blakes and the real estate agent. Selina my darling, perhaps you had better energize the ball for me."

Running to the stable at the side of the dollhouse, Selina released her horse, Nino. She took the crystal ball from Mama and jumped up onto Nino's back. Together they began circling the dollhouse. Round and round the little horse galloped, snorting happily while Selina held the crystal ball high in the air. Rising up onto her toes, Selina stood on the horse's back, balancing perfectly even as the horse went faster and faster. The crystal ball glistened and sparkled like a diamond. It appeared to have a life all its own vibrating inside.

The rest of the Picolinis stood in the doorway of their house applauding each time Selina rode past them. Tonino sulked, miserable at having failed his family.

"*Bravissima,* Selina," called Papa.

"*Perfecta!*" noted Grandpapa.

"*Benissimo,*" pronounced Mama. "You have done well. Now give it to me!"

Selina tossed the radiant crystal ball to Mama. Slowing Nino to a walk, she let the horse cool down before putting him back into his stable.

Mama carefully placed the crystal ball on its stand at the lace-covered table. Passing her hands over the shining globe, she made strange throaty sounds. Soon she looked up with a proud smile. "There, now. I have something for you to see. Look!"

Inside the crystal ball, as clearly as if on a TV screen, the Picolinis saw the Blakes and the real estate agent on the second floor of the house across the street, about to open one of the bedroom doors. The doll family watched in silence as the Blakes suddenly jumped back in horror. A dreadful rumbling, like the snoring of a giant, shattered the stillness of the old house and seemed to frighten both the real estate agent and the Blakes. Even the Picolini family was shocked by the bizarre moaning sounds.

The terrible noise faded away and left a silence so heavy it could almost be felt as it flooded through the house. Both families relaxed a little. The agent found her voice. The Picolinis smiled as they watched her stutter, "P-p-probably the wind. It s-s-sounded like it came from the h-h-heating ducts." The poor woman was desperately trying to reassure both the Blakes and herself at the same time.

"Could be," agreed Mr. Blake, more composed. Embarrassed at having shown even the slightest bit of nervousness, he said in a firm voice, "Let's continue." The Picolinis watched eagerly as Mr. Blake opened the door to a large bedroom. Deeply carved moldings separated the faded wallpaper from the ceiling. The fireplace was lined with blue and white painted tiles. Like a period room in a museum, it was perfectly furnished in the style of the 1860s. The four-poster bed, although covered with a thick layer of dust, was neatly made up with a handwoven coverlet and embroidered pillows. A faded lavender dressing gown casually draped over a chair gave the impression that the occupant of the room had merely gone out for a walk and never returned. Ivory combs and brushes waited patiently on the dresser for someone to use them again.

Mrs. Blake came into focus on the crystal ball, opening a closet and exclaiming over a row of old-fashioned high-button shoes. "Just like mine," said Mama, lifting the hem of her satin dress to show off her own gracefully heeled black patent leather shoes.

Jessica was seen next, holding her father's hand tightly. The Picolinis watched intently as the little group continued. Although the Blakes were still jumpy, they were irresistibly drawn to see the rest of the rooms and the perfect furnishings of the old house. They almost seemed to have forgotten the unpleasant sounds that had disturbed them just a few moments before.

On the third floor, they stopped in front of another closed door. Peter tried to open it, but unlike the other rooms in the house, this one was firmly locked.

Ruth took out her large ring of keys. "One of these has got to fit," she said as she tried one key after another.

"That is the room Florence Bartlett always kept locked!" said Mama Picolini in a most serious voice.

"It's the room Harvey never got to see!" Jessica was saying.

"She's opened it," Mama said. "They're standing at the doorway looking in. Jessica, bless that brave child, is going inside!"

The Picolinis cheered as Jessica dropped her father's hand. They watched her take a small step inside the bedroom. And then they heard Jessica let out a bloodcurdling scream! She had walked into what seemed to be a giant cobweb.

With his Swiss army knife, Peter cut down the elabo-

rate network of fine threads that had prevented Jessica from entering the room. Mrs. Blake took a handful of the web and was examining it closely. "These are old silk sewing threads," she was saying to the others. "This web was obviously man-made, but why would anyone have done such a thing?"

The Picolinis looked from one to the other. "Why, indeed!"

"It's the kind of trick we might pull," said Tonino, staring into the crystal ball.

"Or someone like us," said Papa thoughtfully.

"It was done to prevent us from entering this room," Jessica was saying. Marching bravely into the room, she said, "And you want us to believe this place isn't haunted!"

The Picolinis giggled as the flustered real estate agent scratched her head. Poor Ruth couldn't explain the web of threads as easily as she had the other strange occurrences. Clearly rattled, she busied herself with opening the old-fashioned slatted shutters that covered each window. Daylight filtered into the room, making everything look less grim.

"I can hardly stand the suspense," said Mama, fanning herself nervously with her ivory fan. "If the Flossie and Roberto dolls exist, then they must be in that room!"

"Shush, Mama darling. We can't hear what Jessica is saying," said Papa.

The Picolinis watched silently as the four Blakes stepped cautiously inside the room. "We must be the only human beings besides Florence Bartlett to have walked into this room in over seventy-five years," Jessica was saying.

Suddenly the crystal ball began to shake and tremble. Flashes and sparks burst from it, almost shattering it.

Mama tried to steady the ball with her hands. "It has never done this before," she said in a worried voice.

"What do you suppose it means?" asked Tonino.

"Look! Look! I see what it means!" said Mama triumphantly as the crystal ball focused on the mantelpiece in the room. There, standing demurely under a glass bell jar, were two six-inch dolls dressed in wedding outfits.

"Flossie and Roberto!"

"After all these years!"

"I can hardly bear it."

"Aren't they beautiful!"

And indeed, the two tiny dolls were lovely. Flossie, dressed in an ivory satin wedding gown covered with stars and spangles, held a bouquet of the tiniest silk roses in one arm while her other arm was linked lovingly through the handsome Roberto's. Elaborately dressed in a formal black satin and velvet cutaway suit, he gazed down at Flossie with a look of everlasting love. His famous muscles bulged through his white satin shirt. Their finery, although worn and faded like everything else in the house, still had an air of elegance.

"So there," said Tonino, grabbing three pewter plates and juggling them happily. "I did see shadows. And they were like us. It was Flossie and Roberto! They crisscrossed those threads around the room in order to protect themselves from intruders. Flossie and Roberto made the shadows!" He tossed the plates one by one to Papa.

"You were right, my boy. You most certainly must have seen Flossie and Roberto. When we looked for them in the telescope, they must have been back under that jar on the mantelpiece," said Grandpapa.

"We apologize for doubting you, Tonino," said Papa, sending the three plates sailing back to Tonino. "And now we will have to bring Flossie and Roberto back into our little group. They belong here with us. Somehow we will find a way. I cannot wait to see the look on their faces when they see us!"

"Yes," the others agreed. "We must rescue Flossie and Roberto!"

Mama was very thoughtful. "I believe I now know why my crystal ball didn't work when I was first looking for Flossie. I was concentrating on the real Flossie Barr and not the doll Flossie. The real Flossie is of course dead, and so I couldn't conjure her up. But the Flossie and Roberto dolls exist, and therefore I could easily see them in the crystal ball. I don't know why I didn't think of that before."

"I never doubted your abilities, Mama darling," said Papa, blowing little kisses as he danced happily around her.

10

FLORENCE
BARTLETT'S SECRET

The first thing Jessica and Peter saw after the threads were cut down and bright daylight replaced the gloom of the third floor bedroom was the bell jar containing the bride and groom dolls. Jessica carefully lifted the dusty glass dome so that she could see them better. Admiring the bride's spangled satin gown, her lace veil, and the tiny silk roses, she whispered, "How beautiful you are!" To the groom she said, "And how handsome you are!" Jessica was so entranced by the two dolls that she barely noticed the small trunks at either end of the mantelpiece.

Peter, however, began to fiddle with the tiny latch on one of the trunks. In a few seconds it was open. He was astounded when he saw that it was filled with miniature circus costumes. There appeared to be a complete wardrobe suitable for a six-inch-high acrobat or dancer. Tiny tights, ballet slippers, and a long satin cape were neatly folded inside the trunk. It wasn't difficult to guess that the little costumes were a perfect fit for the bride doll. Peter opened the other trunk. Brightly colored tights and tank tops, obviously created for the groom doll, were piled inside.

"Jess, look at these!"

Reluctantly Jessica pulled her eyes away from the tiny bridal couple and focused on Peter's discovery. "Why, those are circus costumes!" she exclaimed. "These dolls have circus costumes!"

"Just like our Picolinis!" said Peter.

Mrs. Blake examined the handmade details on the tiny circus outfits. Then she lifted the lid of the normal-sized trunk that sat next to an old Victrola in the corner of the room. There, under layers of crackling tissue paper, she uncovered a real wedding gown of yellowed satin, covered with pearls and spangles. Satin slippers with pearl-encrusted buckles were stored underneath the gown.

"This must be Florence Bartlett's wedding gown! And

I can see that it has never been worn. That must be why she was so secretive about this room. Here in her private world, she may have relived a wedding that never happened. But what's particularly curious," said Mrs. Blake, "is that there also are some full-sized circus costumes identical to the smaller ones in the little trunk. Florence Bartlett may have pretended she was a circus performer!"

While Mrs. Blake and Jessica were admiring the wedding gown, Peter was looking at the bride and groom dolls very closely. "Dad," he said to his father who was studying the marble fireplace, "will you look at these dolls? They look just like our Picolinis. The faces are carved and painted in the same style. They could be part of the same set!"

"They do look as if they were created by the same hand," said Mr. Blake casually. He was obviously more interested in the room's structure than in its contents.

"It certainly is odd," said Mrs. Blake. "But it's probably just a coincidence. The circus magician who made our Picolinis might have made others. There may be a whole circus troupe like our Picolinis somewhere in the world, for all we know."

Ruth couldn't make any sense of what the Blakes were saying. She had a house to sell and wanted to get on with it. "Let's proceed," she said impatiently. "We really shouldn't be touching the things here in the house. If you buy the house, of course you will own everything inside it, but until then I suggest you don't go poking inside trunks. Besides, you haven't seen the kitchen or the cellar."

"Oh, you are right and I am sorry," said Mrs. Blake, quickly closing the trunk. "I just couldn't resist."

Mr. Blake was eager to continue. While the dolls were very interesting, he was fascinated by this remarkably well-preserved brownstone. "Onward," he said, gently moving

Jessica and Peter out of the room. Reluctantly the two children followed their parents downstairs.

The kitchen was below the parlor floor, and looked like it hadn't been updated since the 1920s. A single electric light bulb hung from a cord in the center of the room. An old-fashioned enameled gas stove stood on graceful legs on the worn linoleum floor. A refrigerator, topped by a turban of metal coils, was probably one of the very first electric refrigerators ever made. It stood next to a gray stone sink that looked like it had been installed when the house was built. Peter opened a closet and saw a box held by ropes, suspended inside.

"That's a dumbwaiter," said Ruth. "It was used to carry food upstairs to the dining room or to the bedrooms. See?" She sent the box upward by pulling on one of the ropes.

Peter was about to pull the dumbwaiter down into view again when the light bulb began to flicker. As though someone was playing with the light switch, it went on, off, on, off, on, off. The Blakes stood motionless.

"Old wiring," Ruth was quick to say. "I told you it would need complete modernization!"

Mr. Blake nodded. He realized that the electricity would have to be completely redone, but what a unique house it was! He was already itching to draw up plans for the renovation. And these peculiar noises and odd occurrences would disappear when the house was fixed up. It was a great challenge, and since the price was within their range he was almost sure that he wanted to buy the house. He kept these thoughts to himself as they all trooped down to the cellar.

"Wait!" said Peter. "I think I hear somebody down there!" They all stood very still on the cellar stairs as a sound very much like footsteps faded away.

"No one is here," said Ruth. "I am the only one with a key. You are imagining things. Come let me show you!" She boldly continued down the stairs, opened the cellar door, and looked around. Then, satisfied that the cellar was empty, she called to the others to follow her.

Boxes and crates surrounded a wooden table in the center of the cellar, creating what seemed to be a makeshift sitting area. Ignoring it, Mr. Blake examined the furnace and the duct work.

Peter nudged Jessica. "Don't you think it's strange," he asked, "that the whole house is covered with a thick layer of dust, yet this table and these crates are clean?"

"You're right," said Jessica, running her hand over the tabletop and staring at her clean fingers. "This stuff does look as if it was used recently. But who would bother sitting down here when it's so nice upstairs?"

Peter shrugged. Jessica meanwhile wandered cautiously around, stopping suddenly at the front wall.

"Peter!" she cried. "A door!" Unlike the door in their cellar, this one was easy to see. It looked as if it had been opened and closed many more times than theirs.

The agent's eyes followed her finger. "Oh, that," she said. "That's probably the door to the root cellar. Before there was refrigeration, people built root cellars in the earth under the street to keep their vegetables cool and fresh during the winter. Some of these root cellars were made into tunnels for escaping slaves during the Civil War. I wouldn't attempt to go inside to check if this is one of them. They're not safe. They could cave in, since they're very old and haven't been used in years. But a number of these old houses had them."

Jessica was about to open the door of the root cellar when an almost human sounding noise was heard directly above them through the heating ducts in the ceiling.

This was more than Jessica could bear. "I'm getting out of here," she said. "I think this house is haunted!" She ran upstairs, out the front door, and out to the safety of Remsen Street. Peter followed close behind her.

Ruth was apologetic. "I'm sorry the children are upset," she said. "Thinking that this house is haunted is a romantic notion that all old houses seem to invite. Of course we adults know that houses aren't haunted in this day and age."

"Don't worry," said Mr. Blake, as he and Mrs. Blake also started upstairs. "They'll get over it. They'll have to, because I am seriously interested in buying this house! Don't you agree, Amelia, that we could make a wonderful home here?"

"Yes. I'm sure I'll love it. But only after we get rid of those peculiar noises."

"I'm sure there's a logical explanation for everything," said Ruth, as she followed close behind the Blakes.

Mr. Blake held the front door open for his wife and the real estate agent. "I will have an engineer check out the house as soon as possible to see if it is structurally sound," he said. "Then I will get back to you with my decision."

"Don't take too long," said Ruth. "Remember, those three men want to buy it. They are only waiting for a business deal to come through so that they will have all the necessary money. Not that I want you to feel pressured, mind you."

"The minute I get the report, you will hear from me," said Mr. Blake.

11

RASP, BEEZAL, GRUNT, AND CO.

As soon as the front door slammed shut behind the Blakes and the real estate agent, two dust-covered men emerged from the root cellar of the Bartlett house. One of them yelled hoarsely up the stairs, "All clear!" Then a third man clomped down the cellar stairs. All three men burst into gruff laughter.

"Wouldn't those folks be surprised if they could see us now!" said Beezal, the smallest of the three men.

Plunking themselves down on the crates that surrounded the wooden table, the men began to empty two burlap sacks they had hauled in from the tunnel. Out came an ornate silver coffee urn, a silver vase, and about a dozen silver plates, which they dumped carelessly onto the rough tabletop. Another bag held a scale and a tangle of gold chains.

Beezal wore a yellow plastic hard hat stolen from a construction site. He began to place the items on the scale. His narrow eyes watched the quivering arrow closely as he checked the weight. The second man was Rasp, a thin, bony fellow with tightly curled red hair. Rasp seemed to be in charge. With a grimy stub of a pencil he noted the description and the weight of each piece. The men worked steadily until all the items on the table had been entered in Rasp's small black book.

"Not bad, not bad!" said Rasp. "But not good enough! Three hundred twenty-eight ounces of silver and twenty ounces of gold a day ain't gonna buy us this house."

Beezal took off his hard hat angrily and clapped it on his head backward. "Rasp, we put a lot of stuff down there in the tunnel. You're always pushing us to bring in more goods. We made four hits in two days! We can't do more than that."

"You like this house? You wanna get out from the cellar and sit upstairs like a fancy dude? Well, the Slicker won't give us enough for this junk to buy the furniture, let alone the house."

"We don't want the furniture, Rasp," said Grunt, the third and most silent member of the group, shaking his head as he pulled on one of his bushy eyebrows.

"It comes with the deal. You buy the house, you get the furniture. And of course you want furniture, stupid. What do you plan to sit on up there?"

"The furniture ain't my style, Rasp. That old stuff gives me the creeps."

"You give me the creeps, Grunt. And stop pulling your eyebrow. You want to yank it out of your head?"

"Lay off him, Rasp," said Beezal, putting his hat back on properly. "He's been pulling on that eyebrow for years and he ain't pulled it out yet. Let's get down to more important things, like getting the goods ready for the Slicker. You said he'd be here tomorrow night around nine."

Rasp rubbed the wiry red hairs on his arms thoughtfully. "We have to convince the Slicker that this house is important to the syndicate. He's got to put up the dough for the down payment or that family that was just here is gonna get the place."

"Nah. Not them. We got them too scared. They won't buy a haunted house. Those kids ran out of here screaming. They didn't take to Grunt's moaning and grunting. That was some good tape I made of him sleeping. And it sounded great coming through the heat ducts. Real spooky!" Beezal slapped Grunt on the back. "You ain't been named Grunt for nothing, buddy!"

"Yeah, we scared 'em all right, didn't we, Beezal! I thought putting the player piano on a timer was pretty good. Scared me out of my skull to see them keys go up and down all by themselves."

"That smart-mouthed agent thought she had an answer for everything. Drafts and vibrations. What a joke! You don't look like a vibration to me, Rasp!"

"When the kid spotted the tunnel door, I thought we were done for. Lucky for us she didn't open it, and," he added ominously, "lucky for them too!"

"How's the Slicker getting here tomorrow, Rasp?" asked Beezal.

"I'll meet him at my place, then we'll go down into the tunnel and straight through to here, like we always do. After he pays us, we help carry the stuff back to my place, where he'll have a car waiting." Rasp pulled more burlap bags out of the tunnel. "C'mon, you guys. Help me."

The three men began unpacking and stacking the silver on one side of the table and the gold on the other.

"This stuff won't see Brooklyn much longer," said Rasp as he ran his fingers through the pile of gold chains. "It's on its way to South America in a few days!"

"Yeah, and the Slicker sells it for ten times what he gives us for it!" said Beezal, squinting at his reflection in a shiny silver plate. "He makes out like a bandit," he added, laughing at his own joke.

"We ain't got nobody else to sell it for us. And it has to get out of the country fast. You can say this for the Slicker. He pays on the dot!"

"Stop yakking and let's finish up."

Working in silence, the three men weighed and noted every item in the burlap sacks. Then they stacked the sacks back in the tunnel, and Grunt let out a huge belch. "I'm hungry," he said. "Let's go out and get a pizza."

"All right," Rasp said. "But when we own this house, we can have the pizza delivered!"

"And we can use the front door instead of the tunnel. Them tunnels make me nervous. They could be dangerous, you know."

"Nah," answered Rasp. "You just been listening to that real estate agent! What does she know? They've been here for over a hundred years. Why would they suddenly be dangerous?"

"I don't know, Rasp," answered Grunt. "But I wouldn't like to be using them too much longer. I'm glad we'll be buying the house and we won't have to go through the tunnels anymore."

"Those tunnels make the greatest hiding place," said Rasp, pulling down the sleeves of his leather jacket.

"Hey, Rasp," said Beezal, "you gonna let us put our names on the front door like the fancy people do?"

"Yeah, sure. Won't it look great! In brass, 'Rasp, Beezal, Grunt, and Company!'"

"Why does your name always have to be first, Rasp?" asked Grunt. "I think it would sound better if it was 'Grunt, Beezal, and Rasp!'"

"Oh, shut up!"

12

TRAPPED

"Back to your places on the double!" shouted Papa. The crystal ball showed Jessica and Peter rushing across the street. "They'll be here in a minute. Hurry!"

In a frantic scramble, the Picolinis resumed their former positions. Mama, in her excitement, dropped her silk shawl on the floor. There was no time to pick it up before the children entered the apartment.

"No matter how wonderful it is," Jessica was saying, "how can we live in a haunted house where the piano plays by itself and the clock chimes without anybody winding it?"

Peter nodded in agreement. "I wouldn't want to live in a house where weird noises float through the heating ducts and doors slam by themselves and lights flicker on and off and on and off until you feel like . . . like . . . like . . ."

"Like there's a ghost following you!" finished Jessica. "And what's more, I think the ghost doesn't want us to buy that house!"

Mr. Blake entered the apartment. "Look," he said, "I

can understand your fears about the house, but I am sure that all these occurrences will have a logical explanation. I am calling an engineer to inspect the house. He will no doubt solve these little mysteries. And I promise you I won't bid on the house until we hear the report."

"I have simply fallen in love with the place!" said Mrs. Blake. "Just think, a house of our own. I could have a studio and your father could have a workroom. You children would each have a lovely big room of your own instead of the tiny bedrooms you have now. We would have such an exciting time renovating and restoring the house. I'm all for buying it!"

"Hold on a minute, Amelia," said Mr. Blake, "we don't own the house yet. I can't make an offer until the house has been inspected, and the agent did say that there is someone else interested in the place."

"Then, we should have that inspection done as soon as possible. Don't you have someone at your office who could do it?" asked Mrs. Blake.

"I certainly do," said Mr. Blake, "I hope I can catch him in."

Even though it was late on Saturday afternoon, the engineer who worked in Mr. Blake's architectural office was still there and agreed to come over as soon as possible.

"Good," said Mrs. Blake. "Now let's not talk about the house until we have more facts. And kids, since Dad and I are going out for the evening, I've left chicken soup on the stove. All you have to do is heat it up and add some pasta when it boils. And make a salad. Jessica, are you listening to me?"

Jessica was standing in front of the dollhouse, staring inside. "Yes, chicken soup and salad," she mumbled as she reached in and picked up Mama's shawl. "That's strange," she said, draping the little shawl around Mama's shoulders.

"I know I put it on her before we left the house. How could it have come off!"

"Jess, maybe our house is haunted, too," said Peter teasingly. "Really, you probably meant to put the shawl on Mama and just never got around to it. Or it fell off. It's nothing to make a big deal of."

To his mother, he said, "Don't worry about us. We'll get supper when we're hungry."

"Good," said Mr. Blake. "And remember, you are not to open the front door to anyone. There have been a number of burglaries in the neighborhood recently. We can't be too careful."

After Mr. and Mrs. Blake had gone out, Peter tried to reassure Jessica—and himself. "Dad is probably right. There must be a good explanation for all those noises. I really hope so, because it would be neat to have a whole house to live in. And we would get the bride and groom dolls!"

"Those dolls really looked exactly like the Picolinis. And they had all those circus costumes. I'm sure they belonged to the original Pico family. I'll bet they were all part of one big set. Wouldn't it be great to own them? But suppose we don't get to buy the house?"

"Then we don't get the dolls!" said Peter.

"Unless . . ." said Jessica, thoughtfully.

"Unless what?" asked Peter.

"Well, we could . . . rescue those two dolls so that we could keep them with the Picolinis, where they belong!"

"You mean, steal them?" asked Peter, appalled at his sister's suggestion.

"It wouldn't exactly be stealing. Suppose the dolls were once part of the Picolini set. Shouldn't they be returned to their original family? Wouldn't old Grandpapa Pico want them all together? You may think I'm crazy, Peter, but I can almost feel Mama and Grandpapa Pico urging me to get those dolls!"

"Oh, since when can you speak with the dead?" laughed Peter.

"I'm not speaking with the dead, I just have a funny feeling that someone, somewhere is pushing me to get those dolls."

"Jess, no matter how much you think those dolls should be with the Picolinis, and no matter who is urging you to get them, we can't just take them from the house they have been kept in for so many years. Anyway, how could we get them? We haven't got a key to the house."

"What about that door in the cellar? We have a door in our cellar. You said they all connected to a central tunnel."

"You mean we should explore the tunnels to see if they were really part of the Underground Railroad and not just root cellars for vegetables? I wouldn't mind knowing more about those tunnels. If they really were part of the Underground Railroad, what a great report I could make for school!"

Jessica nodded. "We could take a little look down there, and then if the tunnels did connect with each other, we could easily get into the haunted house through the door in the cellar. Then we could get the dolls, bring them back here, and compare them to our Picolinis. If they really matched up, we could offer to buy them from whoever gets the house."

"Suppose the people who buy the house don't want to sell them?" asked Peter.

"Didn't the real estate agent say that the other people interested in the house were businessmen who wanted to use the place for a headquarters? What would they want dolls for?"

"Okay," said Peter. "Are you brave enough to crawl

through a tunnel? You didn't seem to be able to stick around in the house when you thought it was haunted."

"Oh," said Jessica airily, "I just couldn't take any more of those strange noises. I wasn't prepared for them, so they scared me. I admit it! Now I feel prepared for anything that might happen. I'm game to try it if you are." Jessica was trying very hard to sound courageous.

"Okay," said Peter, "if you really think you can do it, let's get started."

"Now?" asked Jessica, beginning to wonder if maybe she had spoken more bravely than she felt.

"Now!" said Peter firmly, grabbing two flashlights from the hall closet and leading the way downstairs to their cellar.

In the dollhouse, Mama Picolini quickly set her crystal ball to work. "Those children are doing a most dangerous thing," she said. "Nobody wants Flossie and Roberto back more than we do, and I confess that I have been secretly willing Jessica to try to find a way to rescue them, but I never meant to have the children put themselves at risk by going through the tunnels to get them!"

The Picolinis gathered around Mama and watched intently as the children marched into the cellar. They saw Peter pull the little door until it creaked open. They saw Jessica walk down the wooden stairs into the narrow tunnel and step gingerly over the skeleton of the dog as she flashed her light in front of her. They watched as Jessica illuminated the roof of the tunnel, and they could clearly see the rotting wooden boards set across the top of the posts that supported the earthen tunnel.

Peter hesitated a moment before he followed his sister. He had to bend low so that his head would clear the roof of the five-foot-high tunnel. The Picolinis heard Peter call, "Jess, not so fast, wait for me."

Then, horrified and helpless, they heard a rumbling and the crashing sound of earth falling. The noise almost shattered the crystal ball.

"*Dio mio,*" screamed Mama. "The tunnel has caved in! The children are trapped inside it!"

13

HELP!

"Will they die?" asked Selina anxiously.

"Are they buried in the dirt?" asked a worried Tonino.

"Their voices must have set off the collapse," said Papa. "Vibrations from a voice have been known to shatter glass."

"Quiet, please," Mama whispered nervously. "I must adjust the crystal ball. I seem to have lost the children. All I see is a pile of earth."

"Find them, Mama darling. You must!" pleaded Papa.

Mama uttered her mysterious throaty noises. Her hands floated back and forth like butterflies as she rocked and swayed in a deep trance, her eyes closed. Finally she looked up triumphantly.

"They are alive! A bit shaken up, but very much alive. Thank heaven."

The Picolinis crowded around the magic ball and saw Peter and Jessica staring in horror at the wall of dirt that had come tumbling down behind them.

"We must aid them," said Grandpapa. "Think of something!"

Helplessly the Picolinis looked at one another.

"We can't dig them out, that's obvious," said Tonino as he looked at his two tiny hands.

"We can alert their parents," said Selina hopefully.

"We could leave a message for them," said Mama.

"A message for the parents! Good idea," said Grandpapa. "How?"

Papa looked thoughtfully over at Mr. Blake's computer. "I have watched Mr. Blake often as he worked his brilliant machine. And I have marveled at the ease with which even the children have learned to use it. Why, they even leave messages for each other on its glass face," he said.

"Do you think you could . . . ?"

"It's terribly complicated, but if you help me, I just might be able to figure it out," Papa said.

In a flash, Papa, Tonino, and Selina spiraled down the leg of the table which supported the dollhouse. Dashing over to the computer stand, Tonino shimmied up its chrome legs, with Selina close behind him. Grandpapa, despite his concern, had to chuckle at the unusual sight they made: two Victorian dolls from the 1880s standing next to a marvel of twentieth century electronic technology!

There were several books standing on the table. Tonino poked among them, sliding out first one, then another until he found the one he wanted. "The *User's Manual,* will that do?" he called down to Papa.

"That's it!" answered Papa. "Send it down!"

Tonino dragged the big spiral-bound book over to the edge of the table.

"Watch out below," he shouted as he and Selina gave the book a hefty push that sent it sailing down to the floor.

Papa grabbed the cover of the book and pulled it open. He turned several pages until he came to the instructions he was looking for. The print was so large for him that he had to walk on the page, bending over each word, slowly spelling them out as he read them.

"Turn on the master switch," he called to Tonino and Selina. "That's this one." Selina pointed to it. Tonino planted one foot against it and pushed the red button until it lit up. He opened the upper disk compartment and bent down to peer inside. "There's something in there," he called down to Papa.

"Good," Papa said. "That will be the word processor disk. Mr. Blake always leaves it there. How about the other disk compartment?"

"Empty!" said Tonino.

"Then take a new disk from the box on the table and slip it inside," instructed Papa. "I watched Mr. Blake prepare that whole box of disks for use. 'Formatting,' he called it!"

Papa then told Tonino what keys to press to set the computer in the proper mode.

"Now, Selina, it's your turn."

Arms held high for balance, Selina walked gracefully on her toes over to the keyboard. Stepping lightly, she carefully danced on the keys until *TUNEL* appeared on the screen.

"It doesn't look right. You must have spelled it wrong," shouted Grandpapa from the dollhouse.

Selina stepped back onto the keyboard. She added an *L,* making it *TUNELL.*

"Still looks wrong. Try again. But hurry," called Grandpapa anxiously.

Selina looked at the screen thoughtfully. There was just one more possibility. Stepping on the delete key, she eliminated the *L* and added an *N*. Papa and Tonino applauded as the correct spelling of the word *TUNNEL* appeared on the screen.

"If the children weren't in trouble, I could enjoy more of this," said Selina.

"Come down now," said Papa. "You did very well!"

Reluctantly, Tonino and Selina slid down from the computer table. "Someday, Selina," said Tonino, "when the children aren't in trouble, we can come back and have some real fun with this machine. I see enormous possibilities here!"

At the edge of the dollhouse, Grandpapa had let down a rope. Tonino climbed up first, and then he helped Grandpapa hold the rope steady for Papa and Selina.

"Oh, no!" said Papa as he climbed back into the dollhouse. "I left the *User's Manual* on the floor."

"Too late. It must stay there. The Blakes should be back very soon. We can't take the risk of being caught outside the dollhouse," said Grandpapa.

"Indeed," sniffled Mama. "I sincerely hope the Blakes will be back shortly. I fear for those children. Somehow I feel as though it is my fault that they are trapped in the tunnel."

"There, there, *Mama bella,* we all wanted Flossie and Roberto back," said Grandpapa. "Who knew the tunnel would cave in? It has been standing solidly for years and years!"

"That's just it," said Mama. "The real estate agent warned them about the danger in those tunnels and we heard it. Their parents told them not to go into the tunnels. Yet we chose to ignore their advice in our desire to get Flossie and Roberto back. And the intensity of my desire made Jessica and Peter forget the warnings."

"Everything will be all right. I know it. Mr. and Mrs.

Blake are due home any minute and they will see our message and rescue the children," said Papa soothingly.

"I only hope you are right," Mama said as she dabbed her eyes with her lace hanky. "I could never forgive myself if anything happened to those dear children." She went back to her crystal ball to keep watch. The others solemnly gathered around.

14

INSIDE THE TUNNEL

Peter and Jessica knew they were now completely cut off from the door to their own cellar. "We're just lucky the dirt didn't fall on us," said Peter, checking to see that Jessica was okay.

"Will we be buried alive down here?" asked Jessica. She fought hard to hold back her tears.

"We'll get out somehow. There should be a central tunnel. And our tunnel should lead right to it," said Peter, trying with all his might to appear brave.

"How could such a cave-in happen after all these years?" asked Jessica.

"Maybe our voices did it. Or our footsteps. Just before it happened, I yelled for you to slow up. That may have set it off."

"Then let's whisper," said Jessica, flashing her light ahead of her, and starting out very gingerly. Jessica had the awful feeling that the narrow walls of the tunnel were getting even narrower.

Peter followed behind. "Even though we have to walk single file, let's stay close together," he cautioned his sister.

Jessica thought about the bones of the dog at the entrance to the tunnel. "Will anyone ever find us if we can't get out?" she whispered. "Or will we end up as another pile of bones!"

"We'll make it. You'll see. In fact, look ahead of you," said Peter, aiming his light in front of Jessica. "It's a tunnel crossing this one! I was right. This must have been part of the Underground Railroad. And this is how the slaves walked their way to freedom!" Peter was so excited he almost forgot to be afraid.

Jessica's flashlight made monstrous shadows on the dirt walls. "I wish it wasn't so dark and damp down here. The earth smell is so strong I can almost taste it."

"Look over here, Jessica," said Peter, shining his light up and down one of the wooden supports which held back the earth. "There are initials carved into the post. See!" He read, "*ZB, JB, X, X, TR, X!* The *X*s must have been made by those who couldn't write their names."

"I can't get excited by some old initials carved into a post when our lives are in danger. I just want to get out of here," said Jessica.

"I want to get out of here, too, but it's still exciting to discover a historic site. Now, there should be a tunnel from the house across the street leading into this one. Look carefully," he said.

Jessica's flashlight played up and down the walls. "We've come to the end of our tunnel. We have to go right or left."

"Try the right," said Peter. "The house across the street is a little to the right of ours and anyway, they may not have dug these tunnels exactly straight. They were digging with primitive tools and in the dark, you know."

The moment Jessica took a few steps into the main tunnel, she saw the entrance to another tunnel! She forgot herself and began jumping up and down in excitement. Peter quickly stopped her.

"We don't need another cave-in."

"Peter, this has to be the tunnel we're looking for. It must be from the house across the street."

"I certainly hope so. I keep thinking that Mom and Dad will be coming home and they won't have a clue as to where we've gone. They'll be awfully worried. If only we had left them a message!"

It pained Jessica to think about her parents. But at the prospect of getting out, she marched ahead confidently, with Peter close behind her.

Suddenly a thunderous noise overhead caused the two children to stop, terrified. Frozen with fear, they held their breath. Slowly the rumbling moved on, fading completely.

"Probably from the street overhead," said Peter, when he felt it was safe to speak again. "Doesn't it feel weird to have a truck drive right over you!"

"Trucks and cars have been going up and down Remsen Street for years. How come cave-ins haven't happened before?"

"It must have been just a freak situation. Maybe my voice just made the perfect sound to start things moving. Or maybe it was about to happen anyway, and our footsteps just helped it along."

Jessica continued walking. She figured that it wouldn't be too long before they would be at the door leading to the cellar of the house across the street. The dampness and chill were making her tremble. She grabbed her brother's hand, and they walked ahead silently when suddenly they stumbled into something blocking their way.

Flashing their lights down they saw several well-stuffed burlap bags piled in the tunnel.

"Don't bother with those things, Jess. Look ahead of
you!"

Jessica almost cried with relief as she spotted the flight
of wooden steps leading to a small door.

"It's the door we want! It has to be!" Shoving the sacks aside, Peter's eye caught something gold at the top of one of the bags. Bending to examine it, he gasped as he saw jewelry, candlesticks, plates, clocks, watches, and small statuary.

Jessica pulled open the top of another sack. "These must be the Bartlett family valuables," she whispered.

"More likely a stash of stolen goods," said Peter as he saw at least a dozen candlesticks, and a mound of gold chains. "Dad said there have been lots of robberies around here lately. I bet we have stumbled into the thief's hiding place!"

"We can't think about all this stuff now. We have to try that door," Jessica said.

Together they shoved their weight against the wooden door. They almost fell into the cellar as the door surprised them by flying open easily.

It took only an instant for Jessica and Peter to flash their lights around and see that they were indeed inside the haunted house. The wooden table and the crates around it stood in the middle of the cellar, just as they had earlier in the afternoon.

Peter closed the door to the tunnel, and the two children ran upstairs to the third floor bedroom. Fortunately, the real estate agent had left the door unlocked.

There on the mantelpiece, smiling as if expecting them, were the bride and groom dolls. Lifting the glass cover, Peter carefully put the groom into his pocket while Jessica tucked the bride under her sweater.

Down the staircase they ran, directly to the front door of the house. Peter unlatched the lock and the door opened easily. The two now stood on Remsen Street in the rain-cooled night air. Peter stopped for just a moment in the middle of the street. With his flashlight he searched the blacktop surface for cracks. There were none.

"What are you looking for?" called Jessica.

"Just wanted to see if the cave-in down below caused any damage up here. The network of water pipes running under the street must be strong enough to hold the street up. The tunnels must be below the pipes."

Peter grinned as relief flooded through him. They were safe. He dashed across the street to where Jessica stood waiting for him. In seconds, the two children were back in the safety and quiet of their own apartment.

"Jessica," said Peter, "I didn't want to worry you, but now I can tell you. We did something really foolish. And I was scared down there in that tunnel!"

15

A MESSAGE TWICE RECEIVED

Peter and Jessica sank into the comfortable cushions on the couch in their own living room.

"I've never been so happy to be home," sighed Jessica.

"You can say that again," said Peter. "But what an incredible discovery we've made! That tunnel has got to be part of the Underground Railroad. We might be the first people to enter it since the runaway slaves used it in the 1860s. Everyone who studies the Civil War hears about the Underground Railroad. But who can say they have actually been in a secret part of it! I can't wait to tell my teacher about this."

Peter pulled the groom doll out of his pocket and handed it to Jessica. Taking the bride out from under her sweater, Jessica looked at the dolls lovingly. "We may have made history tonight, but the best part for me is having these dolls, even for only a little while. They're so beautiful! I hope we can keep them."

"Let's get supper, Jess. I'm starving!"

Jessica stood the dolls inside the dollhouse. "Picolinis," she said, "here are some visitors for you."

Then she turned to Peter. "Now I'm ready for some of Mom's chicken soup!"

The children weren't aware of the fact that their parents had arrived home about half an hour earlier. Not finding their children in the house, and seeing that dinner hadn't been touched, they became quite alarmed. When they saw the computer instruction manual lying on the floor and the word *TUNNEL* on the screen, they assumed that the children had left a message for them.

"Oh, Christopher," cried Mrs. Blake. "All that talk at lunch about tunnels and the Underground Railroad was too enticing! They have gone to explore the tunnel!"

Rushing downstairs, they found the tunnel door hanging open. Mr. Blake stepped cautiously onto the wooden steps that led inside. "I can't believe they would actually go into this dark hole," he said, feeling nervous twinges himself. At the entrance to the tunnel, Mrs. Blake held a light so that he could see.

A few seconds later Mr. Blake realized that the tunnel was blocked off with mounds of freshly piled dirt. He rushed back up the wooden stairs to find a shovel. Fortunately some old garden tools stood near the cellar's back door. He began digging frantically. The light held by Mrs. Blake shook as she tried to hold it near her husband.

Meanwhile, upstairs, Jessica was calmly taking a package of alphabet pasta out of the kitchen closet.

"I used to love these when I was little and learning to read," she said, running her fingers through the tiny letters in the package. "I'm glad Mom still buys them. By the way, Peter, aren't we lucky that Mom and Dad haven't come home yet?"

"What do you mean, haven't come home yet," said Peter as he noticed the coats his parents had tossed over a living room chair. "Not only have they come home, but look at the computer! They left a message for us on it. All it says is 'TUNNEL.' That must mean that they are downstairs at the tunnel looking for us. Oh, my gosh. We have to hurry."

When Jessica realized what Peter was saying, the package of alphabet pasta fell from her hands, spilling all over the kitchen counter. "Oh, Peter, they must be so worried. We better go down right this minute and tell them we're here." She ran out into the hall with her brother following after her.

Rushing down to the cellar, they found their mother holding the light as she frantically encouraged their father to keep digging. "Don't you think I ought to call the police?" Mrs. Blake was asking.

"We're here!" said Peter, timidly.

Mrs. Blake turned with a look of relief on her face. "They're here," she yelled joyously to Mr. Blake. "They're standing right here in front of me!"

Mr. and Mrs. Blake were overjoyed that the children were safe and sound. They hugged and kissed them excitedly before finding their voices.

"It has got to be part of the Underground Railroad," Peter was explaining as they all trooped upstairs.

"We went all the way from our house right to the haunted house. We got out of the tunnel through the little door in their cellar," Jessica said.

"When I saw that wall of earth, I was sure you kids were trapped. I'm so glad to see you alive and well that I'm not as angry with you as I should be. You were specifically told not to go into those tunnels. You knew they could be dangerous. You did a most foolish thing," said Mr. Blake.

"It was pretty stupid," said Peter. "I know this sounds crazy, but somehow I felt compelled to explore that tunnel. It was as if I didn't have a choice. I never even thought about the dangers. I just had to go. But what a report I'll be able to write for my history class!"

"It was so cold and dark down there," said Jessica. "But somehow I wasn't too afraid. Now that I think about it, I realize how silly we were. And I also felt that I just had to go into the tunnel. I didn't even think about the dangers. I'm sorry we upset you. We were just going to get our dinner when Peter saw your coats and we realized that you were home."

By now they were back inside their apartment. Mr. Blake was busy deleting the message "TUNNEL," which he thought the children had left on the computer. As Jessica

and Peter watched, they thought that their father was delet-ing the message he had left for them. There wasn't any question in anyone's mind, so nobody said a word about it.

"Nobody with an ounce of sense would urge you to go into that tunnel, Peter. If anything, we all told you *not* to go into it," said Mr. Blake.

"Let's all sit down together while you kids eat your supper," Mrs. Blake said, setting out bowls and spoons for the children.

"I almost forgot to tell you about the sacks," said Jessica, as she gathered up a handful of alphabets to drop into the chicken soup that was now boiling away on the stove. "We stumbled on some sacks at the entrance to the cellar door across the street."

"Bags and bags of candlesticks and jewelry and little statues," said Peter, as he arranged slices of cheese and tomatoes on bread for sandwiches.

"The tunnel was probably used for a storage room," said Mrs. Blake. "That must be worthless junk you saw stored down there. But we can talk about that tomorrow." Mrs. Blake poured out two steaming bowls of soup for the children.

"I'm not so sure it was old worthless junk in those bags. It sure looked shiny and new to me," said Peter, be-tween mouthfuls.

"We think it was a hiding place for stolen goods," sug-gested Jessica.

Mr. Blake listened thoughtfully. "We'll look into it later. We've had enough excitement for one evening."

"We'll clean up the kitchen tomorrow," Mrs. Blake said. "It's quite late and you must be exhausted. I know how tired I am. You had better go upstairs before you fall asleep down here." Jessica answered her with a sleepy yawn.

As the children trotted upstairs to their bedrooms, Peter nudged his sister. "We're going to have to put the bride and groom dolls back, you know."

"I know," answered Jessica. "But not for a day or two. Nobody will miss them. We have to compare them carefully to our Picolinis. I only got a quick look when I put them in the dollhouse. They certainly seemed to fit right in with the Picolinis. Now don't think I'm silly, but they seemed to make our dolls look . . ." Jessica struggled to find the right words, "even more . . . alive!"

"I don't think you're silly, Jess. I got a quick look at them, too, and I know exactly what you mean. It's as though the Picolinis seemed to perk up when you put the bride and groom inside. But that doesn't mean we can keep the dolls. Tomorrow we'll take just enough time to study them carefully and compare them. Then we'll return them."

"This time, Peter, let's go through the front door!"

16

A GRAND REUNION

In their entire history, the Picolinis had never had such difficulty keeping silent. What joy they felt to see Flossie and Roberto after so many years! Tensely they waited for the family to go to bed so they could move about and speak without being seen or heard. Straining mightily to contain their excitement, they could only gaze adoringly at Flossie and Roberto, who were too stunned to do anything more than marvel at the remarkable turn of events.

Finally, Jessica and Peter went upstairs to bed. The Picolinis hoped that Mr. and Mrs. Blake would follow close behind.

Mr. and Mrs. Blake sat calmly at the dining table, lingering over their tea. "I wonder about those sacks of valuables the children stumbled over," Mr. Blake was saying. "There have been a number of burglaries in the neighborhood lately. Do you think, Amelia, that there might be a connection?"

Mrs. Blake nodded. "I didn't want to alarm the children, so I made light of it. But, Christopher, how on earth could anyone get into those tunnels?"

"Well, a burglar could get in from the house upstairs, through a back window perhaps."

"Christopher, the house has been empty for years. It is just brimming full of valuable antiques. How could a thief operating in the tunnel below the house ignore them! Yet everything seems to be in place. One could tell in a minute if anything was missing by the clean spot in the thick coat of dust that covers everything."

"True, but perhaps they were saving that house for last, since it was such an easy target!"

"Next time we're over there we can examine the sacks. Then we can decide what to do about them," said Mrs. Blake. "I'm more interested in hearing what the engineer has to say about the condition of the house. I hope it's a good report. I can just see us over there, living quite comfortably in all that wonderful space!"

"The report comes in Monday," said Mr. Blake. "I only hope those businessmen won't put in a bid before then. You do understand that we have to wait for the report to know what kind of problems the house has before we buy it. We wouldn't want any expensive surprises later on."

"Of course I understand," said Mrs. Blake, getting up to put the teacups in the sink. Glancing briefly at the messy kitchen with alphabet pasta scattered all over the counter, she assured herself that she would clean it up in the morning, when she was fresh and full of energy.

Mr. Blake rose too. He turned out the lights in the dining room, and they went upstairs to their bedroom.

Barely a second after the Picolinis heard the Blakes close their bedroom door, they sprang into action. Laughter and tears, hugs and kisses all mixed together as they welcomed Flossie and Roberto.

"Put me down, put me down," squealed Mama as Roberto tossed her high in the air. Flossie grabbed Selina's hand and together they rose on their toes and pirouetted gracefully around the dining table. A loud whinny from the stable made Papa run out to release Nino, the white pony. Tonino, seeing that a parade was in order, got out the musical instruments from the attic. He gave a piccolo to Mama, a drum to Grandpapa, cymbals to Flossie, a baton to Selina, and a violin to Papa. For himself he got out his wooden stilts. Slipping his feet into them, he began wobbling awkwardly around the dining room until his head bumped into the crystal chandelier that hung in the center of the ceiling. As if joining in the merriment, the chandelier tinkled gaily as it rocked back and forth. Laughing at his clumsiness, Tonino marched out the front door of the dollhouse. Selina hopped onto Nino's back and led the rest of the family outside the little house. Roberto hoisted Flossie to his shoulders and marched behind the others.

"It's just like old times! Did you ever think anything like this would ever happen again!" said Roberto, smiling up at Flossie. She banged her cymbals merrily in response.

Round and round the dollhouse they pranced, tooting and blowing their instruments joyously. Finally breathless, Mama went back inside, sinking happily into her red velvet armchair. The others followed, exhausted but glowing.

As Selina put Nino back into his stable she looked warmly at Flossie. "I want to hear about everything that has happened since we saw you last!"

Flossie laughed. "That would take years and years, my sweet friend. I promise to tell you all I can remember on long winter evenings."

"We have been rescued none too soon," said Roberto. "There are some rogues who are trying to buy the house we have lived in so quietly all these years. We were afraid that if they succeeded in their plan, we would have been destroyed. The only things these evil characters value seem to be made of gold or silver."

Grandpapa pulled thoughtfully on his white mustache. "That is one story you must tell us about immediately. As you know, our friends the Blakes are also trying to buy the house. Not only do I want the Blakes to get the house of their dreams, but for selfish reasons it is important to us that they get this particular house."

"That's right," said Mama. "The Blake children feel guilty about bringing you two over here. They are already planning to return you. The only way we can all stay together is if the Blakes become the rightful owners of the house and its contents. Since I am not prepared to lose you ever again, it is simply imperative that we prevent those awful men from buying the house before the Blakes are ready."

"They are hard to stop, I'm afraid," said Roberto. "We tried to scare them away by making the house seem haunted. We spent hours stringing a network of sewing threads back and forth across our room. We intended to scare the men away. Instead we only succeeded in giving those three wicked characters the idea to make the rest of the house seem haunted also. We certainly didn't mean to scare those brave children who brought us over here!"

"I saw you through my telescope! You were flitting back and forth. Then when I wanted the others to see you, you suddenly stopped," said Tonino. "They thought I was trying to fool them! I was even beginning to think I had imagined what I saw!"

"So you were responsible for the web that Jessica walked into! But weren't you confined inside a glass dome?" asked Papa.

"A bell jar has no bottom. I easily lifted it high enough

for us to pop in and out whenever we wanted to," said
Roberto, flexing his famous muscles.

"Those three men are thieves. They have a tiny apartment up the street in the basement of another house. One
day, when they were running from the police, they discovered a tunnel in their cellar. It led them to our house.
Finding it abandoned, they began using it as their headquarters. They stored their loot in the tunnel and had their
meetings in the cellar. We heard them talking about it as
they walked through the house," said Roberto.

"They were careful not to take anything from the
house, so as not to make the real estate people suspicious.
They didn't want to lose their hiding place. Besides, they
thought they would get to own everything in the house
anyway when they bought it. They would have owned us,
too, and probably would have used us for firewood!" said
Flossie with a shudder.

"So Peter was correct in thinking that the sacks held
stolen goods," said Selina. "He is so smart!"

Tonino glanced at Selina with a sly smile, as a delicate
blush covered her face.

"When the thieves realized that the house might be
sold to someone else, they went to work in earnest to scare
people away. They thought up some spooky effects, better
by far than our puny threads."

"Like making the player piano start all by itself. And
flickering the electric lights on and off. And winding up the
clock so it would chime," said Papa.

"And sending terrible noises through the heating
ducts!" added Tonino.

"Why yes! Exactly! However did you know all this?"
asked Flossie. Roberto took Flossie's hand gently as he saw
the Picolinis all smiling. "Remember, my love, Mama
Picolini has a crystal ball!"

"You mean you all knew about the timer that made the lights flicker on and off, and the tape recorded noises?" asked Flossie.

"Dear child," said Grandpapa, "we didn't know exactly how they did those tricks, we merely observed them in action. And we saw Jessica and Peter run back here in a dreadful fright!"

"So," said Roberto, "if we want to prevent those men from buying the house, we have to do something very quickly. We heard them talking. They are expecting a person they call 'the Slicker' tomorrow night. In return for all their stolen goods, the Slicker will give them a large amount of money. They know they can't go to a bank and get a mortgage like honest people, and they intend to use this money for the purchase of the house.

"Then we must get Mr. and Mrs. Blake to call the police before those evil men get enough money together to make a bid on the house. We only have until tomorrow night before the thieves meet with the Slicker," Roberto concluded.

"We have no time to lose. We must immediately think of a good way to warn the Blakes," said Papa. "After all, it will be one of our most important communications!"

17

A MOST IMPORTANT COMMUNICATION

"There's always the computer," suggested Selina, remembering the pleasure of dancing on the keyboard.

Papa shook his head. "While it worked very well the first time, the second time might make them suspicious."

"There's a dictionary on the bookshelf," said Tonino. "It has thousands of words in it. We could cut out words and paste together a message."

"No, no," said Papa. "The Blakes would be furious when they found their dictionary all cut up!"

"We could write a poem," said Mama. "We are so good at it!"

"We are good at everything we do, *Mama bella*," said Grandpapa. "However, a poem will take too long. We must do something more quickly."

"We could will them to call the police," said Selina. "Mama did such a good job when she willed Jessica and Peter to rescue Flossie and Roberto!"

"Willing works when you attempt to reach young people. It is a great deal more difficult when you try it with adults. They are simply not as receptive," said Grandpapa.

"You know," said Mama thoughtfully, "the Blakes did not clean up the kitchen after the children's dinner tonight. While I do not approve of such housekeeping, it may come in handy."

"How can dirty dishes come in handy, *Mama bella*?" asked Papa.

"Never mind the dishes, *caro*. What about the alphabet pasta!"

"The alphabet pasta! Splendid! We can spell out a message right on the kitchen counter," said Tonino. He ran out of the dollhouse and spiraled down the table leg as fast as a spinning top.

The Picolinis, Flossie, and Roberto watched Tonino run across the living room to the kitchen. They held their breath as he shimmied up the slippery chrome leg of the counter. They breathed more easily when Tonino finally climbed onto the Formica top. Pushing all of the pasta letters aside, he created an empty space on the counter. Then he began to assemble the letters he needed. Soon he had pushed enough letters around to spell *CALL POLICE HURR*.

"Come back, Tonino," called Mama. "What's taking you so long?"

"I can't find a *Y*."

"Surely with all those letters there is a *Y*."

"There may be, but I can't find it," said Tonino.

"Improvise, *figlio mio*. Use a *V* and an *I*," suggested Mama.

So Tonino searched for a *V* and then added a stem made from an *I*. While it was a different size from the other letters, it completed the word *HURRY*.

Tonino admired his work for a moment, then he scat-

tered some of the letters in and out and around the message
so that it almost looked as though the words *CALL PO-
LICE HURRY* had fallen into place by accident.

Satisfied with the job he had done, he quickly slid
down the side of the counter to the floor below. He ran
across the living room and climbed up the table leg and
back into the dollhouse where he joined the others, who'd
been watching his progress from the attic. Crowding
around him, the Picolinis praised him with slaps on the
back, hugs, and kisses.

Embarrassed by all this attention, he grabbed Selina
and hoisted her up onto the high wire that stretched across
the attic. Selina walked expertly across, calling Flossie to
join her.

"I'm so out of practice, do I dare attempt it?" asked
Flossie timidly.

"You can do it! And I will be below you just in case you need me," Roberto assured her.

Flossie hitched up the sides of her long wedding dress and tucked them into her satin belt. Tossing her bridal veil to Mama, she climbed up the rope ladder to the high wire.

The Picolini family cheered as Flossie, her wedding bouquet held high in the air for balance, walked cautiously, then with more confidence, across the length of the high wire. Bending down quickly, she let the wire slip under her knees so that she hung upside down, arms still out-stretched. Roberto caught her and flipped her to the ground.

"A tower, a tower! Let's make a tower," shouted Tonino.

"Just like the old days," said Grandpapa, twirling his mustache happily as Roberto bent down on one knee so that Tonino could climb onto his shoulders. Flossie hopped onto one of Roberto's outstretched hands. Selina stepped onto his other hand. Slowly Roberto rose to his feet, a mighty tower of strength as Flossie, Selina, and Tonino steadied themselves. Rising onto their toes, Selina and Flossie slowly pivoted on Roberto's palms.

Mama, Papa, and Grandpapa gasped as Tonino put both hands on Roberto's head and flipped into a hand-stand. He, too, began to pivot slowly.

What a sight it was! Roberto held the three acrobats steady as they picked up speed until they whirled around and around. Then, one by one they jumped down and bowed triumphantly in front of their appreciative audience. Mama's red curls swayed as she clapped her tiny hands. Papa danced a merry jig around the proud acrobats.

Grandpapa grinned with pleasure as the group settled down. "This is getting to be quite a party," he said. "But perhaps we should wait until we see that we have something to celebrate. Remember, the Blakes don't own the house yet!"

"You are quite right, of course, Grandpapa. But there is no harm in having some fun! We have done the best we could, and now we must wait for results."

"Hush! I hear noises from upstairs. Back to your places!" said Papa.

Daylight inched its way across the Blakes' living room. Mr. Blake padded quietly down the stairs. He poured himself some orange juice and then suddenly stared in amazement at the kitchen counter.

"I don't believe this!" he said out loud.

Peter, coming down the stairs, said, "What don't you believe, Dad?"

"Come over here and see for yourself! Is this your work or Jessica's?"

Peter rubbed his eyes sleepily. Was he still dreaming? Or did he really see the words *CALL POLICE HURRY*?

"I didn't do it, Dad. And I don't think Jess did it either."

"Then who did it?"

"Maybe they just fell out of the package that way," said Peter although he knew he didn't believe that.

"Letters don't fall into place so neatly," said Mr. Blake. "Someone had a hand in this!"

"Well," said Peter slowly, "remember what the woman who used to own the Picolinis said when we bought the dollhouse?"

"What was that?" asked Mr. Blake, staring at the letters.

"She told us the darnedest things would happen around the Picolinis. Maybe this is one of those things!"

"Don't be ridiculous, Peter. And what are you doing down here so early in the morning, anyway?"

"I couldn't sleep, Dad. I guess I couldn't stop thinking about everything that happened yesterday."

"I know, Peter. My head was full of thoughts too. Especially about those sacks you discovered in the tunnel. Something tells me that they are related to the rash of robberies in the neighborhood. Maybe we should heed this message and call the police right away."

"I think you're right, Dad. And fate or whoever it was who put those letters here thinks so too! I am more sure than ever that Jessica and I walked into a burglar's hideout. Maybe some other family will get robbed while we're waiting for a chance to examine those sacks. Something tells me that there is no time to lose. We could even be the next victims!"

"That's true. And if we are wrong about the sacks, it won't be the first time the police have gone on a wild goose chase."

Mr. Blake went to the phone. He related as much as he could to the police and then put Peter on to tell the rest of the story.

When he had finished, Peter walked over to the dollhouse.

"You all look so smug," he said. "You almost look like you know who messed around with the letters," Peter said with a laugh.

The little doll family looked just as they had when he had last seen them. They stared innocently off into space. The bride and groom stood where Jessica had propped them, gazing adoringly at each other.

Mr. Blake came over and put his arm around Peter. "Let's go upstairs and get whatever sleep we can. We'll probably have a big day again tomorrow, and we'll need all the rest we can get."

As soon as they were alone, Papa, seated on the velvet sofa, sighed with relief. "We did it," he whispered. "The police have been notified!"

18

THE CAPTURE

The police acted quickly. Early Sunday morning a detective arrived at the Blake apartment. Peter and Jessica took him down to their cellar where the door to the tunnel still hung open. Seeing the pile of earth that blocked the way, the detective turned to the children. "I don't think I have to warn you not to enter one of these tunnels ever again! And whoever owns the place ought to block up that tunnel right away."

Tears filled Jessica's eyes as she realized that they might have been buried underneath that mound. Peter put his arm around her and stared down at his feet. He couldn't understand how they had allowed themselves to be so foolish. Had they really been urged on by some unknown force?

"I'd like to take you kids over to the house across the street and have you show me the tunnel over there so that our men can examine it," the detective said.

The real estate agent was there already, waiting with the keys to let them in. She seemed confused by what was happening. She was especially upset by the fact that the front door was unlocked. "I know I locked this door yesterday afternoon. And I'm the only one who has keys to this house!" she said.

Peter and Jessica looked at each other. They knew who had left the door unlocked.

Down in the cellar, the bulging burlap bags were still piled at the entrance to the tunnel, just as Jessica and Peter had said.

"A lot of people in Brooklyn are going to be happy to get their valuables back," said one of the policemen, lifting out a silver coffee urn. "Looks like the family heirlooms described in a lot of our recent complaints are right here in these sacks!"

The detective was poking around the heating ducts. Pulling out a tape recorder, he said, "This may account for those noises you say you heard."

Upstairs, the police examined the player piano. Pulling out a timing device, the detective smiled. "That's all it took to make it play by itself. See!" He advanced the timer to match the time on his own watch. In a few seconds, the piano began to play strange music all by itself. Now that the mystery had been explained, the children were fascinated by the machinery that caused the keys to move up and down as if by magic.

Leaving everything in place in the house, the detective led the Blakes and the real estate agent outside. "We'll be taking action on this matter right away. We'll let you know how it turns out. Meanwhile, thank you for the tip."

Back in the house, the police set up a plan to catch the thief with the stolen goods. Leaving everything exactly as they had found it, they went into the kitchen and hid themselves in the pantry cupboards. The very same heating vents used by the burglars to broadcast the frightening tapes would now transmit with great clarity every word said down in the cellar.

The policemen waited patiently all day. Finally, at exactly 8:30 in the evening, three men entered the cellar from the tunnel. The police heard dragging sounds, which they assumed were the sacks being brought inside. Then they heard the rattling of the candlesticks and silver plates.

At precisely 9:00, the Slicker arrived and they heard the three men greeting him heartily. They waited quietly while the men weighed the loot. They heard the Slicker click open his attaché case. The next sounds were the thumping of the bundles of cash as they were dumped onto the wooden table. At 9:23 P.M. they heard the words, "Count it!" At 9:24 P.M., the police dashed downstairs to the cellar below.

Within seconds, the police handcuffed the four surprised men and took them, along with the sacks of stolen goods and the case full of cash, down to the police station.

The precinct captain was overjoyed. This was indeed the group that had eluded them for so long. "Better tell the Blakes that we apprehended the perpetrators," he ordered a young officer. "They should be the first to know."

When the doorbell rang that evening at the Blake apartment, the Picolinis were sitting tensely in their house, unable to use their crystal ball because the Blakes were in the living room. Although they were very sleepy, Peter and Jessica refused to go to bed until they heard what had happened across the street.

"Did you catch the crook?" asked Jessica the moment she saw the officer's blue uniform.

"We certainly did, young lady. Four of them. And it is thanks to you and your brother that we discovered their hiding place! The captain will no doubt be thanking you personally."

Jessica blushed. She found it hard to be praised for doing something that she knew she really shouldn't have done. At least some good had come out of their bad judgment. She couldn't wait until the next day when she and Peter would ask the real estate agent to let them put back the bride and groom dolls.

"Were these the guys you thought they were? The ones the detective said have been burglarizing the neighborhood lately?" asked Peter.

"There's no question about it. We have someone checking out the stolen items right now. They match the claims we have had these past few months. You won't have to worry about them anymore. They'll get a nice stiff sentence," said the officer. "The only thing we couldn't understand was a remark made by one of the burglars as we removed them from the house." The officer shook his head as though still trying to figure it out.

"What was that?" asked Peter.

"He looked back at the front door of the house and said, 'There goes our fancy nameplate!' Now what could he have meant by that?"

Peter turned to his father, thoughtfully. "Dad," he said, "do you suppose those men were the ones trying to buy the house?"

"Could be," said Mr. Blake. "Obviously they would be very interested in keeping their hiding place from being sold to anyone else."

"Well," said the officer, "I'll be getting back to the station now. The captain wanted you folks to be the first to know. In the morning, after we take some pictures, we'll be removing those devices the burglars set up to scare away potential buyers."

Jessica turned to her mother. "Then the only thing we have to worry about is whether we will actually be the ones who get to buy the house. Now that we know it isn't haunted, I really hope we get it!"

"Me, too," Peter echoed.

"We'll worry about that tomorrow! The report from the engineer should come in sometime in the morning. And now, you both know what I'm about to say," said Mrs. Blake.

"It's bedtime!" said Jessica and Peter together.

19

A WEDDING AT LAST

"I thought they would never go to sleep!" complained Tonino, watching the last slivers of light disappear from the upstairs bedrooms. It wasn't until after midnight that the Picolinis were able to move about.

"They are very excited, my dear boy," said Grandpapa, getting up to stretch his stiff legs. "After all, it isn't every day that they help catch a pack of thieves. Also, they are facing the prospect of buying a house. That in itself would be enough to make them stay up late!"

"True," nodded Papa. "They can be forgiven for being so excited. I remember when Grandpapa Pico presented us with our home back in the 1880s. Ah, it was a day I will never forget!"

"Yes," agreed Mama. "I can clearly recall the day I first set eyes on our wonderful house. I still get a thrill when I sit on our velvet sofa and look at the fireplace with the sweet painting of Sky's End over the mantel. To this day I never tire of looking at the round window with the portrait of Big Billy, my favorite elephant."

"This is certainly a day I shall never forget!" sighed Flossie. "The wonderful day we became one big family again. Poor Florence Bartlett had to leave her circus family forever, but by the most extraordinary set of circumstances I, Flossie Barr, have been reunited with you."

"With me at your side, my dearest," said Roberto, taking her hand.

Mama Picolini looked at the loving couple thoughtfully. "There never was a proper wedding for you two. I do believe the time has come for us to have one!"

"Florence Bartlett held a wedding service for us some seventy-five years ago. She read from her father's Bible, drank champagne, and played circus music on her Victrola. Poor thing. She cried and cried," said Flossie. "It was hardly what you would call a party!"

"Then let us make a real wedding party. A happy wedding," cried Selina, spinning on her toes around Roberto and Flossie.

"What will we use for a ring?" asked Tonino, who had flipped onto his hands and was also circling the bride and groom.

Papa reached into his pocket. He pulled out a tiny gold ring. "This is a link from a gold bracelet of Jessica's. She removed a few of them to make the bracelet smaller. I kept this one, thinking it would come in handy someday. It will make a perfect ring."

Tonino grabbed a tiny velvet throw pillow from the sofa and laid the gold link gently on it. Grandpapa straightened out his jacket and rubbed his gold buttons till they shone. "I shall perform the ceremony!" he said importantly.

Mama got out her lace hanky. "I always cry at weddings," she explained.

"Wait," called Tonino. He quickly spiraled down the leg of the dollhouse table. "There is something I must get!" He dashed across the living room, past the dining table, and into the kitchen. He scanned the shelves of the pantry closet. "Ah ha," he said as he spotted an open box of rice. "Just what we need!" After filling a plastic sandwich bag with as much rice as he thought he could carry, he ran back to the dollhouse, dragging the bag behind him.

Grandpapa let down a rope, which Tonino tied to the plastic bag. As soon as the bag was hoisted up, Tonino quickly climbed back into the dollhouse.

"Wait," called Papa as he, too, slid down the table leg to the floor below. Running to a desk behind Mrs. Blake's easel, he climbed up to the top, where he found himself standing next to a vase of flowers. Rising to the tips of his toes, he pulled out a spray of pink rosebuds and two daisies.

"*Mama mia,* he's taking the flowers Mrs. Blake is using for her still life!" said Mama in a frightened voice. "She'll notice!"

"She'll never miss a few flowers. Look how many are left," called Papa as he scrambled down, with the flowers trailing behind him.

Once again Grandpapa let down the rope. Papa tied the flowers to it so that Grandpapa could haul them up. Then he, too, climbed back into the dollhouse.

"Something old," Mama was saying as she freshened up the silk roses in Flossie's bouquet. "These are now very old!"

"Something new," said Selina, tying a piece of pink ribbon around Flossie's waist and making a neat bow in the back. She had saved the ribbon from Jessica's birthday presents.

"Something borrowed," said Mama, tucking her ivory fan into the pink ribbon at Flossie's waist.

"Something blue. What's blue around here?" asked Selina. The Picolinis ran around the dollhouse searching for something blue. They were determined to fulfill the old saying that for luck the bride should wear "something old, something new, something borrowed, something blue."

Flossie was almost in tears. "We'll run out of time," she wailed.

Roberto looked at Flossie. "Her eyes are blue," he said solemnly. "Won't they do for something blue?"

"Of course! Her eyes are blue! Perfect," said Mama. "Now we can have a proper wedding."

Papa arranged the spray of pink rosebuds in an arch over the front door of the dollhouse. He put a single daisy in the arms of each of the carved wooden bears that held up the columns on either side of the front door. Grandpapa stood in the open doorway, waiting for the wedding procession to begin.

Tonino came first, playing a wedding march on the accordion. Selina, sitting regally on her white horse, followed. Roberto walked slowly behind them, until he stood facing Grandpapa in the doorway. Then Mama walked in, nodding her head majestically as if to a huge and appreciative audience. Finally Flossie floated in, her long wedding dress trailing behind her as she gracefully held Papa's arm. Papa, serious for once, led her to her place beside Roberto. He then stood to one side, next to Mama.

Putting down the accordion, Tonino picked up the velvet pillow with the gold ring on it. With a grand gesture, he held it out in front of him.

In a deep and impressive voice, Grandpapa began, "Dear assembled guests. Using the powers vested in me by an ancient Italian circus family, I am about to perform the ceremony of holy matrimony that will join together Flossie Barr and Roberto Rossi. They are two people who, although married once before in a simple ceremony, have never had the benefit of a wedding party with all the members of their beloved circus family present. Today we are having the wedding that was to take place many years ago, when it was abruptly and cruelly cancelled. Too much time has passed since that terrible day when Flossie and Roberto were removed from us. Therefore we shall not waste another moment!"

Grandpapa cleared his throat. "Do you, Flossie, take Roberto to be your lawful wedded husband?"

"I do," responded Flossie shyly.

"Do you, Roberto, take Flossie to be your lawful wedded wife?"

"I do," said Roberto in a firm voice.

Mama's sniffles almost drowned out Grandpapa's words as Roberto took the ring from the velvet pillow and announced, "With this ring I thee wed." As Roberto slipped it on Flossie's finger, Grandpapa gaily proclaimed, "I now pronounce you man and wife!"

Tonino tossed the rice, as Roberto kissed Flossie tenderly. Hugs and kisses, tears and congratulations followed.

"We need some music!" said Tonino as he picked up his accordion and began playing a lively tune. Flossie turned to dance with Roberto. The Picolinis formed a circle around the beautiful bridal couple. They applauded as Flossie leaned her head against Roberto's chest and sighed, "This is truly the very best day of my life!"

Mama dabbed at her violet eyes and blew her nose delicately.

Papa's painted frown became a tender grin.

Selina giggled and hid her face in Nino's white mane.

Grandpapa beamed with satisfaction. Nothing made

him more contented than seeing joy on the faces of his little troupe.

Tonino looked happily from one member of the wedding party to another. "All we need now to end the most perfect evening is to know whether the Blakes will get to buy the house. Then we can be sure that Flossie and Roberto will stay with us forever."

The little group suddenly grew very quiet. Gloom filled the air of the dollhouse.

"What if . . ."

"Oh, no . . ."

"Wait," said Mama. She reached deep into a pocket in her blue satin dress. Pulling out a deck of fortune-telling cards, she said, "I can foretell the future, if you will just give me a few moments!"

Spreading the little cards out on the lace-covered table, she studied the brightly painted pictures. She topped one with another, turned over a few, rubbed her hands on some, blew on others, and stared intently at them for several minutes.

Flossie and Roberto clutched each other. They simply had to stay with the Picolinis. They couldn't bear to be separated from them again.

Mama dealt out five cards. "One card for each member of the Picolini family!" Pulling out two more cards, she solemnly said, "One each for Roberto and Flossie."

The next card was face down in her palm. "This card holds the answer! I hardly dare turn it over." Lifting the corner of the little card, she barely peeked at it. Then a huge smile covered her tiny face as she exposed the whole card and flipped it down on the table.

"Yes, my darlings," she shouted. "The Blakes will get the house and we will get to stay together forever and ever!"

Grandpapa beamed as the entire group shrieked with

joy and clapped their hands. Glancing at the flowers and the rice-strewn floor, he thought of the clean-up that would have to be done before morning. Twirling his mustache merrily, he shrugged and said, "On such a wonderful night, even cleaning up will be a pleasure!"

A special note to the reader:

While all the known tunnels under the houses in Brooklyn Heights have been closed off, I wish to make it very clear to everyone that should another tunnel, still open, be discovered, it should not be entered. It would be extremely dangerous to do so.

—Anne Graham Estern

ANNE GRAHAM ESTERN has been an art teacher, a scenic artist, a scenic designer, a doll designer, a project director at the Brooklyn Museum, an art director, and in recent years a producer of children's television programs.

Anne Estern's first book for young readers was *The Picolinis* (available in a Bantam Skylark edition). Its sequel, *The Picolinis and the Haunted House*, was written in response to letters from young readers who wanted to read more about the Picolini dolls and their owners, the Blake family. Research into the network of underground tunnels carved out beneath many of the houses in Brooklyn Heights suggested the plot. These tunnels were assumed to be part of the Underground Railroad, which assisted runaway slaves during the Civil War period. Although the tunnels are blocked off now (because of the obvious dangers of cave-ins), Ms. Estern took the liberty of keeping one tunnel open for her story of *The Picolinis and the Haunted House*.

Anne Estern and her husband, Neil, who is a sculptor, divide their time between an old farmhouse in Connecticut and an even older brownstone in Brooklyn Heights. They have three grown children.

HAL FRENCK has illustrated a number of covers of books for adults. This is his first work for a book for young readers. He lives in Connecticut.

Magical Skylark Adventures!

Shop at home
for quality childrens books
and save money, too.

Now you can order books for the whole family from Bantam's latest catalog of hundreds of titles, including many fine children's books. And this special offer gives you the opportunity to purchase a Bantam book for only 50¢. Here's how:

By ordering any five books at the regular price per order, you can also choose any other single book listed (up to a $5.95 value) for just 50¢. Some restrictions do apply, so for further details send for Bantam's listing of titles today!